P9-DNV-854

The world can't get enough of Miss Seeton

"A **most beguiling** protagonist!"
New York Times

"Miss Seeton gets into wild drama with fine touches of farce … This is a **lovely mixture of the funny and the exciting**."
San Francisco Chronicle

"This is not so much black comedy as black-currant comedy … **You can't stop reading. Or laughing**."
The Sun

"**Depth of description and lively characters** bring this English village to life."
Publishers Weekly

"Fun to be had with a **full cast of endearingly zany villagers** … and the ever gently intuitive Miss Seeton."
Kirkus Reviews

"Miss Seeton is the **most delightfully satisfactory character since Miss Marple**."
Ogden Nash

"**She's a joy!**"
Cleveland Plain Dealer

Witch Miss Seeton

A MISS SEETON MYSTERY

Heron Carvic

This edition published in 2017 by Farrago, an imprint of
Prelude Books Ltd
13 Carrington Road, Richmond, TW10 5AA, United Kingdom

www.farragobooks.com

First published by Geoffrey Bles in 1971

Copyright © The Beneficiaries of the Literary Estate of
Heron Carvic 2017

The right of Heron Carvic to be identified as the author of this
Work has been asserted by him in accordance with the Copyright,
Designs & Patents Act 1988.

All rights reserved. No part of this publication may be reproduced,
stored in a retrieval system, or transmitted, in any form or by any
means, without the prior permission in writing of the publisher.

This book is a work of fiction. Names, characters, businesses,
organizations, places and events other than those clearly in the
public domain, are either the product of the author's imagination
or are used fictitiously. Any resemblance to actual persons, living
or dead, events or locales is entirely coincidental.

ISBN: 978-1-911440-56-7

Have you read them all?

Treat yourself again to the first Miss Seeton novels—

Picture Miss Seeton
A night at the opera strikes a chord of danger when
Miss Seeton witnesses a murder … and paints a portrait
of the killer.

Miss Seeton Draws the Line
Miss Seeton is enlisted by Scotland Yard when her paintings
of a little girl turn the young subject into a model for murder.

Witch Miss Seeton
Double, double, toil and trouble sweep through the village
when Miss Seeton goes undercover … to investigate a local
witches' coven!

_____

Turn to the end of this book for a full list of the series,
plus—on the last page—**exclusive access to
the Miss Seeton short story** that started it all.

Almost at odds with mourning.
Which is witch?

—*not quite* SHAKESPEARE

Chapter 1

Poor cow.

Chief Inspector Brinton of the Ashford Division stamped cold feet in the damp grass. Five-thirty A.M. was no hour to be up—let alone out. So all right; if farmers liked it, farmers could have it. If they'd the sense they weren't born with they'd get up at a civilized hour. Then if they must find stiffs lying about in their ditches civilized people'd be prepared to take a civilized interest in 'em.

The chief inspector watched as Potter, Plummergen's village constable, crouched against the thorn hedge, with two patrol car men and a couple of farmhands, worked ropes under the body and prepared to ease it out of the deep dike that bordered one side of the field. He turned to the man beside him.

"All right, doc, we'll ship her back to the lab for you and she's all yours. Let's have the report soon as possible, though it looks clear enough. From the marks on the legs I'd say tied up and slit open while still alive."

The other hunched his shoulders. "Wouldn't be so much blood else."

Brinton beckoned to the farmer. "Can your men keep their mouths shut?" The farmer nodded. "Good, see they do.

Yourself as well. Looks like ritual stuff. Things are bad enough as they are, and that Black Mass business at Malebury church hasn't helped, so we'll keep it under wraps for the moment. If this gets out, with everybody seeing witches and devils all over the blasted place, we'll really start something."

He moved away. Religions. They'd had a bellyful of 'em. As if they'd not enough on their plate with this other lark, Nuscience, which had got the chief constable climbing trees. After the Maidstone force on the C.C.'s instructions had tried twice and failed to infiltrate the business and find out what it was all in aid of and why half the richer people in Kent seemed to be handing over their money like lambs led to slaughter, the C.C. had called a confab of the heads of all police departments. Some twit had suggested calling in the Yard. Didn't seem to realize you couldn't hand over a case you hadn't got—and for all they could prove Nuscience might be lily white. Brinton smiled slightly. He'd come up with a suggestion of his own on infiltration and the C.C.'d half bought it—especially as if it came off it actually would bring in the Yard in a backhanded sort of way. And with this witch stuff beginning to look serious they could do with any help they could get on Nuscience. Anyway the C.C.'d O.K.'d for him to go to London and have a word with the Oracle on the q.t. and see what could be arranged. Might try and pick the Oracle's brains on witches at the same time.

Witches. Brinton took a last look at where the men were maneuvering the body onto level ground; glanced down at his shoes, bespattered with reddened mud; scraped them in the grass, making the uppers as wet as the soles; bunched his hands into his pockets and strode back to his car.

Poor old cow.

The chief inspector had had no previous occasion to visit New Scotland Yard. He stared at the building: must cost 'em a bit for window cleaning. He went in; gave his name, rank, address, place of business, proposed business; was handed over to a guide, ushered into a lift and wafted aloft.

Detective Superintendent Delphick rose as his visitor was shown into the office.

"Chris. Good to see you. You know Bob Ranger." He indicated his sergeant.

"How are you, sir?" Detective Sergeant Ranger gathered some papers from his desk and made for the door.

Brinton waved him back. "Sit down, boy. All right, so this visit's not official, but we may want you."

The boy, all six foot seven of him, with breadth in proportion, returned to his place. He put the papers on his desk and sat down with a sinking feeling. What could old Brimstone be wanting with him? The only connection he'd had with Kent, apart from Anne, were those jaunts with the Oracle to Plummergen. Granted but for that he'd never've met Anne. But Plummergen? Surely Miss Seeton couldn't be at it again.

"Coffee or tea?" asked Delphick.

"Thanks, Oracle, coffee," said Brinton.

The sergeant lifted the telephone receiver and ordered coffee and biscuits for three.

"Well, Chris"—the superintendent settled back in his chair—"what can we do for you, and what brings you to town?"

The chief inspector grunted. "Religion." He put a briefcase on the floor and dropped his hat beside it.

Religion? Delphick eyed his old friend. "And your visit's off the record, I gather. Has Canterbury mislaid the Archbishop? What's the trouble?"

"Imported trouble," replied Brinton, "or that's our guess. And your headache—or will be, I hope. Some so-called religious hogwash known as Nuscience with an office address in London." He grinned at the superintendent. "So all right, Oracle, my coming here's unofficial, but with official blessing. And our chief constable's having an unofficial word with your assistant commissioner as well, because of a bright idea I had, since we've already got our hands full with another religious lark."

Delphick was interested. Must be something way out to faze Chris Brinton. "What goes on?"

The other shook his head. "The Devil, an' all his works. We've got an outbreak of tea leaves—not petty thieving—but reading teacups, table rapping, crystal gazing, all that. And it's spreading."

Delphick laughed. "What's so serious about that?"

"You'd know if you had to cope. Black Masses, witchcraft and all that guff. So this other crap that's got our C.C. in a spin, this Nuscience, is one over the odds."

The superintendent made a note. "Any connection between the two religions?"

"No. Except that one feeds the other. With all this hoohah about witches and people seeing the Devil round every corner, they begin looking for somebody else to hock their souls to—while there's time. Witches." He snorted. "You always get a bit of that here and there—mostly harmless, though it seems to be on the up just now—but this Nuscience lark, end of the world any moment, I gather, 's got us beat, and the gulls're flocking to it like wasps to jam. It's a racket, I'll swear. It's so po-faced and pie-eyed it's got to be crooked."

Delphick made another note. "Nuscience … End of the world … There's something there that rings a bell." He thought for a moment. "No—I can't get it. Something to do with Scotland, I think. I'll check."

"And now," continued Brinton, "just to help things along, we've had a killing."

"Killing?" Delphick looked up sharply. "When? I hadn't heard."

"Night before last sometime. Papers haven't got it yet—and I don't intend 'em to. Told everybody to keep quiet. Don't want to start a scare."

The sergeant stared. Had old Brimstone gone off his chump? You couldn't hush up murder; there'd be hell to pay.

The superintendent leaned forward, pencil poised. "Who's the victim?"

"A blasted cow." Delphick put his head down to hide a smile and wrote: *Read up on witchcraft.* "A farmer named Mulcker called us in yesterday morning when he found the remains," Brinton went on. "I've had the vet's report and we've done a bit of probing around, and I don't like the look of it—it's nasty." He described the scene. The farmer, who lived just outside the village of Plummergen, had rung the local constable soon after 5 A.M. The village P.C. had taken a look and called Brettenden, who, on hearing his report, had called Ashford. The crew of a patrol car who had intercepted the call, after a survey, had reported back to headquarters. The chief inspector, in a glowering temper, had been dragged from his bed and forced to tramp wet fields in drizzling rain to view the carcass of a cow. The view had worsened his temper, although it had changed its direction. The body lay in a ditch which bordered a field. The marks of ropes still showed on the fore and hind legs. A rushed autopsy report had confirmed the police suspicions: the animal had been tied and then the heart and liver cut out while it was still alive.

Delphick dredged his memory. "Was your cow a heifer?" he asked.

Brinton gave a grim smile. "All right, Oracle, so you've got the idea."

The superintendent remarked his sergeant's bemused expression. "A heifer, Bob, is a virgin cow. The blood sacrifice of a virgin, as in voodoo or black magic. Refertilization of the ground through the blood of the victim." The sergeant's expression remained bemused. "Have you found any trace of the heart and liver?" Delphick asked.

"I think so." A knock on the door heralded the coffee. Settled again, Brinton took three spoonfuls of sugar and stirred slowly. "I alerted all the local lads to keep their eyes open and Potter, our boy in Plummergen, noticed the ashes of a fire in a corner of the graveyard 'longside the old ruined church beyond Iverhurst—Iverhurst's on his beat, only about a couple of miles from Plummergen. He scoured round, then radioed for us. There were some burnt scraps of offal with the charred remains of thorns still stuck in 'em—or that's what it looked like. Haven't had the lab report yet but I'm pretty sure." He put his cup on Delphick's desk. "Doesn't help," he added, "that Malebury, where they had a Black Mass business two weeks ago, is only an odd ten miles away just over the county line."

"I see." Delphick reflected. "Yes. Not pretty. And once they start killing there's no knowing where they'll stop."

He considered: so far they'd had religion; Nuscience; witch-craft; Nuscience again; dead cows; then witchcraft again. What was Chris really after? "This bright idea of yours you mentioned—what is it exactly you, or your chief constable, want us to do?"

Brinton was suffering from uncharacteristic embarrassment. Down in Kent his solution had seemed the obvious and practical way out of a difficulty. Here in London in a professional police atmosphere it became suddenly far-fetched and amateur, so that now that he had come to his main hurdle he was balking. He looked at the ceiling, at the floor and finally at Delphick. "All right, Oracle, so it's your drawing teacher girl friend, the Battling Brolly." The sergeant heaved a sigh. He'd known it. All along. Anything near Plummergen that had anything as off as sacrificial cows and cooking their innards for supper in churchyards was sure to have Miss Seeton in the back-ground somewhere. Or if she wasn't yet, she would be—he'd take a bet on it.

"What's poor Miss Seeton done?" inquired Delphick.

"It's not what she's done, it's what we want her to do. We want her to join Nuscience."

Delphick sat up. "You want her to what?"

"Our C.C.'s worried. We've been keeping an eye on some of their public meetings round the country—all very orderly and well run, and all very damn silly on the face of it. But it's got a nasty taste. Too many people with money joining, and the C.C. thinks they're being fleeced. So he decided to try a stoolie. Maidstone had a couple of goes but got nowhere. The first, a young detective, went to a meeting at Tonbridge all dewy-eyed and keen but was turned down flat. Their Lord High Muck-a-muck—they call him the Master in Nuscience—told him he hadn't got the right call. My guess is they thought he hadn't got the right cash. The C.C. said all right, so he'd dip into funds, and tried again with somebody older, a woman detective sergeant, who was to ante up the three hundred entrance fee you need to become a Greenhorn, their lowest rank." He grimaced. "And you'd want to be one to pay that to be that. But they're pretty fly—wouldn't touch her. To my mind it was the right idea, wrong woman. She was a tough, intelligent type. What you want is some gullible-looking, dowdy old trout—the sort that goes for that kind of twaddle. And then I thought: Blimey, we've got the very thing. Miss Seeton, she's made to measure."

"Miss Seeton," objected Delphick, "is not a gullible old trout."

"Didn't say she was, said she looked it. A hundred-and-one percent innocent like her—they wouldn't suspect her in a thousand years. Nuscience've got a meeting coming up at Maidstone. She's local. Who more likely to tool along out of interest and then get all of a twit over the tripe they spout and want to join 'em? They aren't to know she hasn't got money. Some of these old girls you get living alone in small cottages are fair stacked."

Delphick shook his head. "I don't see it, Chris. Miss Seeton's got far too much common sense to want to join the sort of setup you describe. How do you expect to persuade her to act as stoolie for you? If you tell her the truth—even if she'd do it, which I doubt—she's no actress and she'd give the show away at once. Besides, if there's big money in this racket, as you suggest, it could be dangerous."

Brinton dismissed this last demur. "Oh, we'd send some-body along with her to see she's all right. For the rest"—he prodded the edge of the superintendent's desk with a stubby forefinger—"we're hoping you'll persuade her."

"Me!" exclaimed Delphick. "Oh, no. You do your own dirty work."

The other ignored him. "You know her better than I do. After all, she's worked for you—you've paid her for odd sketches she's done—very odd, some of 'em." He waxed enthusiastic. "Come to that, we could do it the same way. Tell her we're interested in this Nuscience, need to know a bit more about it, and want a bit of help—she'd fall for that, and anyway it's true enough—and if she'd go along to a meeting and make some notes and perhaps a sketch or two of anything she thinks interesting, and if after the meeting she could even bring herself to join the gang—we'd supply the cash—it might help us even more." He grinned. "Might, at that. Things have a knack of starting up when she's around. I don't say she starts 'em but you got to admit they start."

Delphick shrugged and leaned back in his chair. "Try it if you want to, Chris. If you've got your chief constable sold on the idea there's nothing to prevent you, but I don't see how we come into it."

"Oh, don't you!" retorted Brinton. "That's what our C.C.'s having a word with your Ass. Comm. about—a sort of unofficial hand-over to you of the whole lark. My idea was it's time your colossus here"—he jerked a thumb at the sergeant—"was due for some leave. Since he's engaged to Dr. Knight's daughter, it's time he got himself down to Plummergen and did a bit of courting. We'll be wanting somebody on the spot to keep his eyes open with a reason for being there that needn't connect up with police work."

Leave? Pop down to Kent and have some time with Anne? Bob Ranger glowed. This was the stuff to give the force. He looked hopefully at his superior.

"Why Plummergen rather than Iverhurst?" asked Delphick.

"Iverhurst's too small. Three or four farms, a few cottages, and that's your lot. Not even a general store. Plummergen's no distance with a population round the five hundred mark. If your Ass. Comm. agrees, and Miss Seeton agrees, it means we'll have your sergeant there on the spot with a reasonable cover, to keep an eye on things, to keep you in touch, and also to keep Miss Seeton under control."

The sergeant's eyes widened. He blinked. Keep Miss Seeton under control? There was no such animal. She'd go capering off armed with innocence and an umbrella, and everything'd be backsides-up from here to Land's End in no time flat.

The superintendent dropped his pen back on his desk. "Granted all this, have you checked on Miss Seeton, Chris? What's she up to? Is she free?"

Brinton laughed. "I asked Potter. He tells me that, like the rest of the countryside, Plummergen's got the jitters over witchcraft and half the village have more or less made up their minds that Miss Seeton's the leading witch. From the moment Potter mentioned her and witches it struck me like Fate. I thought, if she's starting up again at least let's start her on the right tack. It'd be a positive kindness to winkle her out of witchery and pop her into Nuscience. God knows, if she'd poke that umbrella of hers into Nuscience and pop that for us we'd be grateful. But if she's going to start midnight baths in ponds again, like she did before, and swimming up and down the canal and generally creating merry hell, I'm not taking the responsibility, not on my own. Besides, we'll need an allocation for hats and — umbrellas—she can run through three a week when she's in form." He chuckled. "So all right, you can't help liking her, but cope with her I can't."

It was finally settled that if Sir Hubert Everleigh, Assistant Commissioner, Crime, was agreeable, Delphick should hold a watching brief for the time being and that Sergeant Ranger should be seconded, ostensibly on leave, to the Ashford Division and stationed at Plummergen, while Miss Seeton should be engaged, if possible, to see what she could make, if anything, of Nuscience.

Chapter 2

She was a doll.

The September sun sparkled on the glass of the window where she sat, immobile, remote; shone upon her hair, which fell to her shoulders in one slow wave of blended gold. Her eyes, glints of blue from a mountain lake in summer, were veiled by half-closed lids and the heavy sweep of eyelashes, while the subtle flush of a ripening nectarine found rival in her complexion. Her nose was small and straight, her mouth a long-drawn coral bow with the deep indentation of the upper above the full sensuous curve of the lower lip. Molded by an expert, her chin showed the suspicion of a cleft. Her figure was concealed by the leaf green of the dress and the turquoise velvet of the cloak tied with a golden cord about her neck. Secret and still, she held attention though she paid none. She was delicious. She was delight itself, irradiant and irresistible. She was a doll.

Miss Seeton entered the shop.

"Eric," hissed Mrs. Blaine, "did you see that?"

"See what?" Erica Nuttel turned from the post office grid at which she was buying stamps and looked around the shop.

"That Seeton woman," said Norah Blaine in an appalled tone. "She bought pins."

"Something slipped?" suggested Miss Nuttel.

"No, not safety pins. Ordinary pins. It's too peculiar."

"Why, Bunny?"

"But, Eric, didn't you see?" Her friend Mrs. Blaine was impatient. "She bought that doll in the window. Well, naturally I wondered. What could she possibly want a thing like that for? After all, it isn't as if she's got any relations—or anyway"—her lips pursed in disapproval—"none that we've ever heard of. Except of course old Mrs. Bannet, who was only distant, and a great pity, to my mind, that she ever left her the cottage, godmother or no." She looked accusingly round the post office and Plummergen's main general store. "I can't think why Mr. Stillman wanted to stock that kind of doll in the first place. Much too sophisticated for a small village like this. Too unsuitable. And," she added, "much too expensive. I thought it was peculiar, but"—her voice dropped, vibrant with outrage—"the pins explain it. It's too dreadful."

"Don't follow."

"But, Eric, don't you remember? The other week in *Anyone's.*" At the summit of her tall, angular frame Miss Nuttel's equine head nodded as the implication struck her. It also struck elsewhere: *Anyone's* was widely read in the village. Mrs. Flax paused in the middle of an argument with Mrs. Stillman as to whether bananas should be served in, or with, curry. Even an animated discussion at the cheese counter on the new Bulman baby and the fact that he did not look like Jack Bulman but was the image of they-knew-who died away. Norah Blaine's plump figure trembled with agitation. "That dreadful article on witchcraft and devil worship. It said there that there were places where you can buy dolls with packets of pins all ready to stick in them. And I ask you: for someone like that to buy a doll like that—well, what other explanation could there be?"

In the present climate of public concern the explanation was reasonable; reasonable for two ladies whose main preoccupation was other people's business and who were untiring in their efforts to explain everybody's actions to everyone else, the criterion of the explanation being the interest it could excite rather than the truth it might contain. A spate of disquieting articles had been appearing in the newspapers advising the public of a serious increase in black magic and witchcraft. Demonology, they informed their readers, was Gaining Ground. The Black Art, aggravated by drugs, was Becoming a Menace. More and more people were sinking below the surface of conformity to Explore the Depths. The trend, they asserted, was worldwide. UNESCO was anxious about the situation in Germany. Australia was apprehensive about Sydney. In New York the authorities were disturbed to find that the tentacles of Obeha were reaching out from the Negro and Spanish-speaking quarters down through York and First avenues toward Sutton Place. This Terrible Cult, the newspapers warned, was Spreading in Britain. Remote country districts, city centers, suburbs and rural villages, they insisted—none could count on complete immunity from the infection. Even in Plummergen the villagers felt that they were under threat. Only a few miles away a congregation had recently been discovered at a Black Mass and routed at Malebury church in Sussex. There were rumors, although nothing had yet been proved, that there was at least one coven in Kent. But rumors, to spread, must have their mongerers, a duty generously undertaken by Miss Nuttel and Mrs. Blaine. Sharing a house, opposite the garage and in the center of Plummergen's only street, through the modern plate-glass windows of which they keep an untiring and speculative watch on the local scene, they publish their own interpretations of such trafficking as they espy. Knowing themselves to be faultless, they make it their mission to detect the myriad faults in others, against which they wage incessant tongue. Strict vegetarians, their meatless condition brings them closer in their own estimation to spiritual matters; to the occult. They had seized upon the present witch scare as a challenge to their powers and had begun a spirited spiritual opposition with table rapping, planchette, teacup reading, palmistry and cards. The craze was sweeping through the village, and tables bounced in many cottages. Among the *Mastery* books in the post office *Master Metaphysics in 30 Minutes* was a best seller.

In the wider world of commerce, enterprising businessmen had realized the possibilities of the situation. Voodoo supplies, dragon's blood, bat's blood, graveyard dust, levitation ointment and wax dolls had become a six-figure industry. It was true, as had been reported in the papers, that at certain shops the dolls could be bought complete with a packet of pins. The doll had to be dressed to resemble the offender and the pins inserted. The operator could then sit back with sublime faith in the happy prospect of the victim suffering pain per pin or even, were the practitioner sufficiently capable, death.

At certain shops? Witchcraft in Kent? No village exempt? The article in *Anyone's* and the press warnings flickered through Miss Nuttel's mind.

"See what you mean, Bunny, but ..." A real witch in a tiny village like Plummergen? The evil eye, Satanic rites, orgies. She was impressed. "Bit awful." She was intrigued. "But when you think ..." She thought. "All that happens when that Seeton's about—murders, burglaries and whatnot ..."

"And nothing ever happens to her," threw in Mrs. Blaine. "Quite."

Mrs. Blaine's enthusiasm mounted. "And then think how she's got the police bewitched."

"Don't like to have to say this, Bunny ..." By now most of the shoppers in the post office who had gathered around the two ladies to miss nothing of the stop-press from this latest edition of the Plummergen scandal sheet held their breath as Miss Nuttel prepared to pronounce judgment. "... wouldn't say it to anybody but you—but you could be right. Explains a lot."

"And to think," wailed Norah Blaine, "of its happening here of all places. It's too dreadful. Somebody ought to do something."

Mrs. Flax, still holding a banana, waved it in emphasis. "You're right, dearie, they did an' all." This support was not free from bias. Mrs. Flax lays out for the village and the fact that she ministers to a mind deceased gives her a certain status; she is held in some awe. A knowledge of herbal lore and remedies adds to the reputation she enjoys and she has come to be looked upon as the local wise woman, to be consulted first as well as last, with the doctor only as an intermediary. For this foreign newcomer to set herself up for a witch was a right bit o' cheek and not to be put up with; putting down was what she needed. "I"—she looked at the company slyly—"could tell you a thing or two about things—things better not to mention. What happened to Ted Mulcker's cow? Broke its back falling in t' dike yester morning, so they say. Likely tale. And if it broke its back why were it slit up and gutted, with blood all over?" A cow? Yesterday? This was particular; immediate. Interest quickened. And Mother Flax would know. Her son worked for Ted Mulcker. "Aye," relished Mrs. Flax, "slit up alive and blood all soaking in the ground. That's sacrifice, that is, and don't let none tell you different." They plied her with questions. Belatedly Mrs. Flax remembered that she was sworn to secrecy. Her son would do her dead to rights if he learned she'd gabbed. She looked virtuous. "There's nought I can say, I'm sworn. But this I will say. If she—naming no names—done that, there's no bounds what she might do next. We're not safe, not none of us. I doubt we could all wake up murdered in our beds and none the wiser." Her hearers shivered in querulous sympathy. "When all's said, she's nought but foreign—from Lunnon or such."

"Exactly," denounced Mrs. Blaine. "She'd never have come here in the first place if she hadn't inherited that cottage. And we don't know what sort of life she lived in London; in fact we know very little about her, which means there must be something wrong."

"I don't see how you can say that," protested Mrs. Stillman from behind the counter. "I think Miss Seeton's been wonderful. Look how she's helped the police—and all of us, for that matter—when there's been trouble." The group turned, surprised. Some wavered. Mrs. Stillman's place was to serve, not to obstruct. Scandal thrives on encouragement, not on opposition.

"Trouble," echoed Mrs. Blaine. "That's exactly what I'm talking about. And who's at the bottom of it? Ever since she came here there's been nothing but trouble—just one thing after another. And," she concluded, "you notice none of it's affected her. How do you explain that if there isn't something odd?" She gave a triumphant glance about her, then her eyes widened and she stared: all turned to follow her regard. Mrs. Blaine's too busy imagination was rapidly carrying her and her audience from the tingle of fancy into the tangle of fantasy. Before their frightened gaze, at the bottom of the shop's center display, a smiling group of painted garden gnomes began to leer. Above the gnomes hung a coil of rope. Witches trussed with rope—for ducking; trussed for burning; witches were hanged with rope. The next shelf held a row of pet food: Pussyfoot, The Kitty's Joy, in tins, each wrapper with its emblem, a black cat. Black cats—the witch's symbol. A bundle of besoms in a corner caught her eye, caught everyone's. She held her breath, so did they all, as the twiggy brooms took on a new and evil aspect, their humble duties now recast to sweep, instead of leaves, the sky. Dolls? Pins? Black cats and witches' brooms? All the paraphernalia of sorcery in their village post office? Had they been misled? Were they, all unsuspecting, at the center of a web? Were vicious practices rehearsed behind closed doors? Did seemingly innocent neighbors only seem so? "We should have guessed before," Mrs. Blaine declared, "with all that's been in the papers. Don't you see? It means there's a witch—a real one, I mean—living right here amongst us." The shop seemed colder. A tremor ran through them all. "And it's no good going to the police; that Seeton woman would only fool them as she always does. What can we do?" She appealed to her hearers.

"Tell 'er to go," was one suggestion.

"Ask the vicar," was another.

Miss Nuttel sniffed. "What's the good of that?"

"We all know she's got old Arthur Treeves in her pocket," said Mrs. Blaine. "And his sister's just as bad. No, we must manage for ourselves." She had an inspiration. "I know. That man at the Nuscience meeting in Tonbridge the other week—a splendid speaker. He'd be the right person. He was talking about the Devil and made it all too clear. He said we must fight evil wherever we can find it, but to fight it properly we must understand. I remember he said we must rise above ourselves and fight on other planes."

"Other planets, Bunny," corrected Miss Nuttel.

Her friend was put out. "Well, I don't see any difference; it comes to the same thing. But he's so impressive and good-looking and I think he's right. He even mentioned witchcraft. It was just after that business at Malebury church—how it was like a bog sucking people down to damnation and was just another symptom of the end of the world. He's exactly the sort of person who could help us. It's a lot of money but I feel it would be worth it. I think," declared Mrs. Blaine, "it's safer to be safe. Yes, I really think, Eric, we should join."

Old Miss Wicks was shocked. She had listened in distress to what was being said about that nice Miss Seeton but had been unable to tear herself away, owing to the fascination of the subject. The newspapers made witchcraft seem so real, such a menace, that for the first time she found that she was nervous of being alone in her little house at night. But Nuscience … That was some sort of new fancy religion. What would the vicar say? Indignation made her unfortunate front teeth appear to protrude even more than usual, producing an even more unfortunate effect than usual of sibilance in her speech. Miss Wicks was scandalized.

"Scandalous," whistled Miss Wicks.

Mrs. Blaine waved this aside. "There's another Nuscience meeting at Maidstone soon; we must go, Eric." She addressed everyone. "I think we all should. We—we ought to stand together. Otherwise anything could happen—things like orgies." Breathless, she turned to the postmaster. "I think I'll take an extra tin of that tomato, raisin and nut soup."

Following her leader's courageous example, Mrs. Flax advanced upon Mrs. Stillman. She slapped her banana on the counter, bursting its skin. "You can keep that. Curry," she huffed. "Heathenish stuff. I'll have no truck with it. Give me two Oxo cubes and a couple of packets o' frozen veg and a tin o' carrots an' I'll make a stew. Healthier"—she looked accusingly at the postmistress, who had stuck up for that foreign witch—"an' safer."

Fear of the supernatural would appear to have stimulated the appetite. Having frightened themselves beyond intention, everyone began to order more than her usual quota of groceries, in the hope perhaps that an excess of normality would of itself induce the norm.

Unaware of the whirlpool she had stirred, Miss Seeton was on her way home. Once outside the post office, she could see her cottage at the end of the Street. It gave her, as it always did, a surge of pleasure and of gratitude; pleasure in the unlooked-for ownership of a charming home, gratitude to the memory of her godmother, who had bequeathed it to her. The cottage, although it stands alone in its own small front garden, is neighbored on either side by the short row of houses which faces down the Street, lending to Plummergen the immediate impression of a cul-de-sac. In fact there are two exits: one a narrow lane running beside the brick wall which bounds Miss Seeton's garden; the other, Marsh Road, is a right-angled turn, invisible at any distance owing to the trees in the bakery garden. Marsh Road leads back north around the marsh to the town of Brettenden and its sign-post, labeled RYE, would appear to have been placed there for the sole purpose of fooling the unwary. Marsh Road is a road: it is sufficiently wide for two cars to pass if they are driven with care. The lane is a lane: it is narrow enough to induce care in any lorry driver who wishes to pass through it without a scrape. It is, however, the lane which is the thoroughfare; a small vessel connecting two main arteries; the link between London and Maidstone, through Brettenden and, once it has debouched onto the bridge over the Royal Military Canal, one of the principal routes to Lydd airport and the coast.

The large garden at the back of her cottage would have proved an encumbrance to Miss Seeton had she not inherited, along with the property, her godmother's arrangement with a local farmhand and his London-born wife. Stan Bloomer looks after the garden in his spare time, grows vegetables and fruit for Miss Seeton, for his family and for sale; he also cares for the chickens in the two hen houses at the bottom of the garden on the same principle. His wife, Martha, comes in two mornings a week to clean, cook and do anything else she deems necessary, for a nominal salary. One thing Miss Seeton had not inherited was the where-withal to maintain this property. Old Mrs. Bannet had left her all she had, but when death duties and the rising cost of living had taken their toll, the resultant tiny income, even when added to her pension, left Miss Seeton in a precarious financial position.

Miss Seeton had been fortunate—or unfortunate, according to the point of view—in that her arrival to take up her inheritance and stock of her position had been attended by a blaze of publicity. It has never been determined whether her history of involvement with untoward events is her fate or her fault. To witness a murder in London was a happening for which she could hardly be blamed, but to poke the murderer in the back with her umbrella during his performance in a praiseworthy attempt to correct his manners was an act which laid her open to criticism. It was an act which had brought her to the notice of Scotland Yard. Her experience as a drawing mistress had enabled her to sketch a recognizable portrait of the killer. Superintendent Delphick had found further of her sketches useful since Miss Seeton sometimes and without intention put down on paper her intuitive feelings about a character as well as, or instead of, a likeness. Later the superintendent, with the permission of the assistant commissioner, had employed her on another case. The experiment had proved successful. Miss Seeton did not know, would never understand, the real reason why the police found her to be of use. She knew that artists were often employed when photographs were unobtainable or impracticable. She therefore thought of herself, when she thought of it at all, as an occasional Identi-Kit drawer, not realizing that for an Identi-Kit an artist was not employed. The checks that the police had paid her for sundry drawings had temporarily eased her circumstances and she had felt justified in indulging the extravagance of buying the doll.

Major General Sir George Colveden, Bart., K.C.B., D.S.O., J.P., owing to his unremitting interest and help in all village affairs, had found himself landed involuntarily with the outmoded role of local squire. He and his wife had taken Miss Seeton under their wing during the difficulties that had attended her arrival in Plummergen, since the consequences of the murder in London had followed her to Kent and had succeeded in involving almost the entire village before the case was finally solved.

Miss Seeton, sensible of Sir George's and Lady Colveden's kindness, had for some time felt distressed that there was nothing that she had been able to do in return. Only a few days previously she had been invited to tea and had met their married daughter and her little girl. Miss Seeton had found them both charming and had been very touched the next morning when the child, Janie, had called at the cottage with a bunch of flowers that she had picked "for your pictures." The mother and daughter were returning to London this afternoon after a short visit and a parting present of the doll could hardly be refused and would, Miss Seeton hoped, give pleasure. She shifted the gift-wrapped box under her other arm for comfort.

"Scuse me, miss." Miss Seeton turned. A small, happily grubby boy studied her with solemn eyes. "Me nuisance's stock up t' tree."

"Your …?" Her gaze followed the indication of a pointing finger. On a branch just out of her reach was a—well, a balloon, she supposed. Four bloated red sausages attached to an inflated orb with an orblet for a head: it resembled the gentleman who advertises Michelin tires. Probably a space man, she decided. Miss Seeton raised her umbrella and gently prodded the object. Carefully she lowered it free of the branch. The child jerked the string. Miss Seeton's umbrella had a sharp ferrule. There was a pop and the body of the figure disappeared; its appendages began to wither, thus metaphorically fulfilling Chief Inspector Brinton's pious hope that she would stick her umbrella into Nuscience and pop it for him. "Oh dear," said Miss Seeton.

"Don' matter," the boy comforted her. "Got 'nother." From a pocket he produced some wrinkled red rubber. He put it to his mouth and blew. Another space man blossomed. Inserting a plug, he untied the string from the corpse and attached it to Mark II. He held it out. "Give that a poke with yer brolly," he suggested. "Makes a good bang."

"Don't be silly," protested Miss Seeton. "Then you wouldn't have a balloon."

"Would an' all. Got three more." He rummaged in his pocket again and held them up. "Me mum's a Nuisance, yer see. She got 'em at a meeting. They gives 'em you for free if yer gives 'em enough lolly to join 'em. It's a 'vertisement, yer see."

"Still I think you'd better make them last as long as you can, otherwise your mother won't be pleased. Also"—Miss Seeton frowned—"you shouldn't refer to your mother as a nuisance. It's not polite and I'm sure it isn't true."

"Is an' all," the boy reiterated. "Me dad's wild. 'E's Railway, yer see, with overtime on t' farm an' 'arvestin' an' such and me mum does field, spuds an' beans like—savin' for a car they was—and then me mum she goes an' swipes the lot an' gives it to this Nuisance an' me dad was that mad I thought 'e'd do 'er straight." His eyes sparkled at the recollection. " 'Sides, 'e's church, yer see, an' 'e don't 'old with Nuisances."

Miss Seeton abandoned the argument. Obviously there was something one hadn't quite understood. The Kentish dialect. So very different for a newcomer. She smiled, nodded and went her way.

Chapter 3

"Something awful has happened." This breakfast bombshell failed to explode. "I said," said Lady Colveden, putting down a letter and taking more butter, "something awful's happened."

Her son raised balanced egg on sausage. "Such as?" He munched.

"Aunt Bray," replied his mother.

Nigel pushed his plate aside and reached for the toast rack. "Dead?" he asked hopefully.

"You shouldn't be callous," his mother reproved. "Though," honesty forced her to admit, "it would be nice."

Nigel spread toast. "Then what's she done?"

"She's coming here."

The explosion lost none of its effect through delayed action. Nigel choked, while the newspaper opposite her went down with a scranch. "No," said Sir George.

"Yes, George." Lady Colveden tapped the letter. "She's coming to stay."

"Put her off."

"I can't. There isn't time. She's arriving this afternoon."

"Tell her we can't have her."

"Don't be silly, George, how can I? And if I did it wouldn't make any difference. You know she never listens unless it suits her."

"Or doesn't suit others," put in Nigel.

"And anyway," concluded Lady Colveden with unanswerable logic, "she's your cousin, George, not mine."

Nigel dug into the marmalade. "What's happened to the juvenile delinquent?"

"Nigel, I've told you before that's not the way to speak of your cousin."

"Second cousin," corrected her son, "twice removed—by the police."

"Besides, Basil wasn't delinquent. If your mother's got as much money as Aunt Bray has, you're maladjusted and go to an approved school."

"Approved by whom?"

"How should I know? I imagine it's a school that approves of that sort of thing. After all," she pointed out reasonably, "I suppose even criminals must be trained somewhere."

Sir George passed his teacup. "Why?"

"Why?" echoed his wife. "Because ... well ... Oh, I see: why Aunt Bray? You'd better hear the worst." She picked up the letter. " 'Dear Margaret' ... Nobody but Aunt Bray has ever called me Margaret. Oh, no, that's all complaints about the servants." She dropped the page. " 'I cannot understand ...' No, that's a complaint about some committee or other. Ah, here we are. 'Since leaving school Basil has got the most wonderful job with some wonderful people, which only shows how wrong George has always been about him. He's got THE FAITH'—I think she must mean Basil has, and it's in capitals—'and so have I. It's changed my whole life, I'm a different woman.' "

"Doesn't sound it." Sir George took his refilled cup from Nigel.

"Well, no," she agreed. "But if the change has only just begun, it probably wouldn't show yet. 'Until I accepted Freedom and grasped the Infinite I hadn't lived. This world is ending very soon now, but we in Nuscience will Go On and carry the Torch Beyond. I'll explain it all better when I see you.' "

"She'd need to," said Nigel.

" 'Basil has become a Trumpeter—isn't it wonderful—and very well paid. We had a wonderful meeting in Tonbridge and next week is to be the final one at Maidstone. After that they will disclose our Secret Place.' "

"Woman's mad," said Sir George.

Lady Colveden skimmed the rest of the effusion. "She says she'll be arriving this afternoon to stay for a few days and go to this meeting, that we must go and that it's wonderful and worth every penny of it. 'But Basil will stay in Maidstone with some of the'—well, it looks like Majordomos but it can't be—'because some people'—she means you, George—'are so unreasonable.' "

"I too," declared Nigel, "am unreasonable. Father only chucked him out of the house. I chucked him into the pond when I was only nine. What is this whatsit meeting anyway?"

"It must be some sort of religious concert," guessed his mother, "if Basil's playing the trumpet."

"Well, count me out," said Nigel. "Aunt Bray's the end and Basil's beyond it, but trumpets'd be the last straw." "Straw!" she exclaimed. "That reminds me. Have we got any clean straw or shavings in the barn?"

"Probably. What d'you want them for?"

"Packing. I must send off that quite lovely doll that Miss Seeton left for Janie. It was such a shame she couldn't give it to her herself; and she really shouldn't have spent so much. But still"—Lady Colveden brightened—"she might find the extra money useful. I had a word with the other school governors and we all said yes."

Sir George folded his paper and stood up. "To what, m'dear?"

"Mr. Jessyp spoke to me the other day; he says it's all very well being called headmaster, but with only one other teacher—and she's always taking time off to visit sick mothers and aunts and cousins and things—he's more of a pen pusher and bottle washer and would the board mind him asking Miss Seeton to do occasional part-time teaching at the school if she could manage it."

"That should teach the tots a thing or two," said Nigel.

"Well, why not?" replied his mother. "After all, crises are a part of life, and you can't deny that Miss Seeton's an expert on crises. Disasters follow her about wagging their tails like friendly puppies and she just pats them on the head and solves all the trouble without even knowing there was any and comes up smiling at the other end. What better education could there be? It's a pity the Government didn't get her to deal with the railway strike yesterday; she'd've sorted it out with one wave of her umbrella and then Julia and Janie wouldn't've had to go home early. I think Miss Seeton should go into politics. They're always having crises there and she'd clear them up in no time with a little common sense."

Sir George turned at the door. "Common sense and politics don't mix, m'dear."

For Miss Seeton, too, there was cause for misgiving in her morning post.

Really. Very kind. And of course in a way, she supposed, gratifying. If one wanted to, that was. Teach, she meant. Miss Seeton laid down the curtain that she was hemming, pushed the box of pins aside for safety and reread the letter.

The School House
Plummergen
Kent

Friday, 26th September

Miss Emily D. Seeton
Sweetbriars
Plummergen, Kent

Dear Miss Seeton,

Further to our conversation the other day, I have been wondering whether you would agree to consider working here occasionally as a part-time supply teacher—nothing onerous, and only when you feel free to do so.

I have an immediate occasion in mind. Miss Maynard has had to visit her mother, who is ill, and will not be returning until next Monday night. If you would take over her class on the Monday I would be most grateful. The work is all set so it would require little more than supervision. Also we have planned an educational visit for the following week to give the children a day by the coast. If you would be willing to accompany them it struck me that this might be combined with an art project; possibly a competition for the best painting of some particular view—to be chosen of course by yourself. The pay would naturally be in accordance with the usual scale for teachers, which, as you are probably aware, is quite reasonable for those doing occasional supply work.

Perhaps you will let me know your reaction.

Yours sincerely,
Martin C. Jessyp

So that was what Mr. Jessyp had meant when he had stopped her in the Street and introduced himself. Now that she thought of it, she did remember that he had particularly asked her whether she had undergone a training course. Well, actually one had. Mrs. Benn, who had always proved so very thoughtful as a headmistress, had especially asked one to. And although one had, in fact, qualified and had, on several occasions, taken over classes from the other mistresses at the little school in London, one could not, one feared, feel it was one's forte. Drawing—well, that, she hoped, she understood. Of history she had perhaps a certain knowledge. But geography … and, above all, mathematics … It was difficult to believe that children could derive any benefit from a lesson in which the teacher knew less than nothing of the subject.

But teaching … If one were honest one had, one was bound to acknowledge, sensed a certain relief on one's retirement as a schoolmistress; at no longer having to teach children who, for the most part—and quite understandably—had no wish to be taught. However, in this instance she could hardly refuse. After all, it would not be often and, there was no question, the money would be helpful. On Monday? That

31

left very little time. She must reply this evening. Just so long as it was not mathematics.

Miss Seeton picked up the second of three letters. The envelope was typewritten and addressed to "MissEss, Sweetbriars, Plummergen, Kent." She smiled. Her code name, of course. It must be from Scotland Yard. But surely it couldn't be a check. They owed her nothing. How very odd. Superintendent Delphick, she felt sure, would have addressed her as Miss Seeton. No, to be accurate—the superintendent was always meticulous in such matters—it would probably have been her full name and initials. How curious. It was quite a problem to imagine what anyone at Scotland Yard could be writing to her about. Miss Seeton finally resolved the problem by slitting the envelope and extracting the contents. She read with surprise and growing dismay. Really it was very kind of Sir Hubert. Most thoughtful. But no. It was quite out of the question. It would be most improper. For oneself, that was. Particularly at one's age. Even if, as Sir Hubert suggested, one was only retained. She was perfectly willing, as Superintendent Delphick knew, to do occasional Identi-Kit drawings: indeed she had been most grateful for the work and the police had been more than generous. But this … She read the letter again. To join the police force? No. Really that would not do. She had neither the knowledge nor the experience for such work. How very strange life was: to be offered two posts in one day. In his letter Sir Hubert reminded her of their meeting on an occasion when she had visited Scotland Yard, and begged forgiveness for using the absurd nickname that the Yard's computer had given to her: it would appear that this monster had its own foibles and among them was a childish dislike of being corrected; so to avoid tantrums and uphold the filing system it was simpler to continue to use MissEss, if she was agreeable. Oh, so that had been the reason. Well, naturally she quite understood. Like her bank in Brettenden when they had gone under—or was it over—to a computer. Sir Hubert also urged her not to answer his letter at once but to take her time and think it over. Sergeant Ranger, he informed her, was on leave and would be visiting friends in Plummergen. The sergeant would avail himself of the opportunity to call on her, with her permission, and discuss her reaction to the proposal. The sergeant ... Such a very large young man, and so, one felt, reliable. The friends, of course, would be Dr. Knight and his family. The sergeant and Anne, although he was so big and she was so small, were, one felt instinctively, a perfect match. It was such a very real pleasure when two young people who were ideally suited met and recognized one another. Miss Seeton sighed with the pleasure of it.

The third missive was a circular. It was headed "CURRENT CUTS." "DO YOU," it demanded in loud capitals, "KNOW WHAT THEY ARE SAYING ABOUT YOU?" Well, really. There must be some mistake. She looked at the envelope again. Yes, it was her name and address, but ... She started to read the accompanying letter.

Dear Madam,
As someone who is constantly in the public eye, would you not be wise to take advantage of our Contemporary Cuttings Service? We cannot, alas, all expect universal praise, but is it not better to know the worst as well as the best? ...

Good gracious. In the public eye? It certainly couldn't be meant for her. She had never, Miss Seeton reflected with mistaken satisfaction, been in the public eye. Nor was she likely to be so. It would be most unbecoming.

Many people have the happy mental knack of banishing matters that do not suit them. Miss Seeton is capable of dismissing from her mind any occurrence in her life that does not conform with her conception of the life of a gentlewoman. Gentlewomen do not, in Miss Seeton's estimation, become entangled in outlandish situations; therefore, in Miss Seeton's view, neither does she. Miss Seeton's view, however, is unique. In the village she is variously regarded as a heroine, as a villainess, as a gentle creature who does her best to avoid the troubles that beset her path, as a termagant who, wielding a lethal umbrella, is always in search of trouble. There is no denying that since her arrival in the locality trouble has frequently prevailed. In banner headlines the newspapers have dubbed her "THE BATTLING BROLLY," though of this she herself is happily unaware. It is true that although crime followed her from London down to Kent, she has also unearthed or stumbled upon crime indigenous to Kent. Of this too she is unconscious, since crime holds no interest for her and she will always attribute where possible the best of motives to anyone she meets. It is in part the fault of the police that her reputation has continued to balloon. Asked by Superintendent Delphick to make one sketch in a case that was worrying him, before the case was finished she made many and went on a spectacular crime-busting spree which landed her back in the headlines; though not the headlines, not the crimes and definitely not the spree have ever been recognized as such by her. Even when forced by circumstances to admit the oddity of some predicament in which she finds herself, she can reject the oddity as an accident which might happen to anyone. In such circumstances she considers that it is one's own behavior that counts: it is important to remain normal and correct. The fact that Miss Seeton's normal and correct behavior in strange circumstances generally leads to chaos is unfortunate and she has always been loath to concede any sequence in the curious events that befall her. To do so would be to recognize a pattern of oddity, and a pattern of oddity in the life of a gentlewoman would not be normal and most certainly it would not be correct. For those around her the question will remain: is she an innocent, tempest-tossed, or does she toss the tempest?

Miss Seeton got up and repaired to the kitchen. She had promised Martha to keep an eye on the jelly bag. Apparently the string and the bag were inclined to stretch during the first hour of hanging and would probably have to be retied a little higher. Yes. Martha had been right. The bag was lower. It was nearly touching the basin. She crossed to the window, dropped the Current Cuts circular on the draining board, reached up to the ancient meat hook set in the beam above the sink and hefted the string. Goodness, it was very heavy, and—she looked down at the liquid in the basin—of a most beautiful color, a wonderful wine red. One had always thought of bramble jelly as nearly black, but Martha had said that that was only when it was over-cooked. Miss Seeton succeeded in retying the bag higher and stood back to admire the effect. It was so much larger than one had expected; it should make a lot of jelly. Now— had she done all that Martha had told her to? Yes, the bag was still directly over the basin, but it was swinging slightly. She steadied it. And it was dripping very slowly. Martha had said the slower the drip, the better the jam. So that was all right, she needn't worry about it anymore, just leave it to hang there until tomorrow morning. The circular caught her eye. Ridiculous nonsense. And, when one considered, perhaps a little rude. She retrieved it, put her foot on the pedal of the waste bin and dropped in the folder. To suggest that people might concern themselves with her affairs. As if they would.

Dressed in dark slacks and pullovers, they stole forward on plimsolled feet. Fired with enthusiasm, upheld by righteousness, Miss Nuttel and Mrs. Blaine had set out upon a mission, prepared to venture all, to explore during darkness the ill deeds of night, in an attempt to prove themselves, to themselves and to Plummergen, as leaders worthy of respect. Spying upon the enemy in their midst, they would show where guilt lay and become the established saviors of the village from the dangers that encircled it. They crouched; they stealthily advanced; they bent beneath the hedge; they peeped above it; then, greatly daring, pushed the gate. It squeaked.

"Eric, what shall we do?" gasped Mrs. Blaine. "It squeaks."

"Give it a shove and get through quick," advised Miss Nuttel.

They did. It squeaked again; but they were through and now deployed, each to one front window of Miss Seeton's cottage. They peered to no avail; shone flashlights, saw their own frightened faces reflected in black glass, peered closer, saw the rooms empty and innocent. Together they tiptoed round the building, looked through the French window; nothing showed; came to the kitchen window and pressed near. They shone their flashlights and pressed nearer still: two noses flattened against a pane of glass, four staring eyes saw—horror. Above a basin hung a monstrous thing wrapped in white cloth, decapitate. It hung there in the dark and as they watched in frozen fascination a globule formed, enlarged, then fell, a glistening ruby drop, into the bowl beneath, already partly filled with—blood. A baby's head hung from a beam; was dripping blood. The witches' prerequirement, blood from a newborn babe, compulsory constituent in all their horrid rites. Two mouths slumped open in soundless screams; two faces fell away, a dropped flashlight clattered. The stumbling, running scamper of distracted feet, the rasping breath of terror, the crunch of trodden flowers, the squeaking of the gate, the slap of rubber soles on pavement as oversized buttocks in undersized pants pistoned the legs.

"Eric," wheezed Mrs. Blaine, "did you see? Too awful. Too … Oh, I shall be sick. How could she? It's too dreadful. But I said so all along. Didn't I, Eric? Eric." She stopped. "Eric." She looked around. *"Eric,"* she wailed. But Eric was not there; she was alone.

Back down the Street, back through the squeaking gate, back around the cottage to the corner where, not daring to go farther, Mrs. Blaine stood trembling, grasping the rough brick wall. Above her a lighted window warned of danger. The light was blocked: a head looked out; it looked this way and that, looked down; a skinny arm was thrust into the night, the hand upturned. In supplication? Calling up spirits from infernal climes? Norah Blaine tried to remember prayers. The hand, its dreadful aim accomplished, was withdrawn.

No—Miss Seeton pulled the window to—it wasn't raining. Well, that was a good thing. Though it was quite cold.

A touch of early frost? One did hope not, for that would spoil the flowers. She was almost sure that she had heard a noise. But no. Everything seemed quiet. It could have been a dog. Or then again, perhaps, more likely, cats. In any case nothing to worry about. She would get back to bed.

Its malediction done, the head retired; curtains were drawn; the light went out. Shaking, Mrs. Blaine began to move. Her flashlight, obscured by fingers, scoured the ground. She found a broken flashlight. She picked it up. She cast again and found Miss Nuttel lying prone, eyes closed, face waxen. Was she dead? Had that vile woman done her worst?

"Oh, Eric, has she killed you?" She felt the pulse. It beat. The body breathed. "Speak, oh, please." She slapped the face. The figure croaked, a guttural sound. A croak? What had that evil woman done? Had she used spells? Was Eric now bewitched? But noise was dangerous. Quickly she laid her hand upon the mouth. Miss Nuttel struggled to sit up.

"Wha—what's going on?" she mumbled.

"Shh," pleaded Mrs. Blaine. "Oh, Eric, please get up. We must—must get away from here while there's still time."

Miss Nuttel focused her recovering mind. Despite a gruff manner and laconic speech, she was always undone by the sight of blood. Between them they got her length erect. Her knees would not support her; she clung to her small and rounded friend, and thus entwined they tottered to the corner of the cottage; they teetered to the front; went weaving down the path—the long and short of it, inarticulated angles balanced on a sphere—and the gate gave one final squeak of protest behind two old hens with staggers on their way home to roost.

Chapter 4

"It was definitely there on the hall table yesterday afternoon; I was in the middle of packing it when you arrived. I can't think what's happened to it; I've looked everywhere. You don't think—Oh, thank you." She helped herself to vegetables. Nigel served his father and himself, put the dishes on the sideboard and returned to his place. "You don't think," ventured Lady Colveden, "that Basil might have picked it up when he brought your luggage in and put it in his car by mistake?"

"Are you"—the turkey neck extended, the reddened wattles wagged, the beaky nose was lifted high—"are you," brayed Honoria Trenthorne, "suggesting that my son would steal a doll?"

"No, no, of course not." Lady Colveden retreated. "It's just that I thought he might have. I mean," she amended hastily, "he might've taken it by mistake; or for a joke or something. Nobody else was there and …"

"Don't be ridiculous, Margaret. My son doesn't play jokes. In any case what could a boy of twenty possibly want with a doll, d'you imagine?"

"Imagination boggles," murmured Nigel.

"Nigel, be quiet." Meg Colveden was worried. "I had it out on the hall table ready to pack. The tissue paper, the wrapping paper, the shavings and the box are all still there, but the doll's gone. I simply can't understand it."

"Ridiculous fuss to make about some footling doll," rasped Mrs. Trenthorne.

"It isn't footling," protested Lady Colveden. "It's a beautiful doll. Miss Seeton brought it here for Janie, but because of the train strike yesterday they'd gone home early and she missed them. I was going to send it on, but now I don't know what to do. I can't tell Miss Seeton; it'd be so disappointing, and she might go and buy another. And I can't ask Mr. Stillman at the post office to get me one; if it got out it would be all over the village and Miss Seeton might hear and that would be awful. I'll have to try and find one in London and make Julia and Janie promise not to tell."

"Seeton?" Mrs. Trenthorne looked down a Roman nose. "Is that that vulgar umbrella woman who's always in the papers? Then I can't say I'm surprised. She probably stole it back herself to get advertisement. It's a mistake to know such people." She turned to her host. "As a local justice, George, you should know better."

"Fiddle," said Sir George.

"There's no excuse to be rude, George, just because I'm family."

Mrs. Trenthorne's family claims were marginal. She was the cousin of a cousin of Sir George. The name Aunt Bray had been bestowed on her by Nigel, who, hearing her raucous voice for the first time at the age of five, had noted the likeness to a donkey's plaint. When told indulgently to kiss her and call her Auntie, he had stood back, fixed her with a look and said, "Aunt Bray." Unaware of its derivation, the lady had assumed the nickname to be a child's expression of affection; a mistake excusable in that she had little experience of affection, given or taken, to guide her. Meg Colveden had seized upon the affection angle, thankful only that her son had not said Auntie Heehaw. Nigel's elder sister, Julia, had endorsed the nickname and thereafter to the Colveden family she had become Aunt Bray, an infrequent and unwelcome visitor. Not recognizing that in her voice nature had given her a foghorn which no one could ignore, she had evolved her own method of gaining the attention of any company in which she found herself. She quarrelled vociferously with everyone she met and if faced with placatory agreement would immediately reverse her views to ensure an argument. She liked, she declared, a good fight; she found it stimulating. She had married money meek and mild whose only recorded defiance had been his retirement to an early grave. Whether her only son's precocious aptitude for petty thieving and later for forging checks was the result of his environment or an intuitive knack was a question for the psychiatrists to answer. He had been alternately described as mentally retarded or advanced according to his mentors' individual opinions, or depending on how much the boy had pinched. Lady Colveden sought to change the conversation.

"Tell me, Aunt Bray, what is this meeting you're going to, and that Basil's playing at?"

Mrs. Trenthorne was affronted. "Playing at? I don't understand you, Margaret. Nuscience is not a game. It's wonderful. For those who believe, it's basic and fundamental; it relates the spirit to the Great Beyond."

"Beyond what?" asked Sir George.

"Beyond this planet, George; beyond this life; beyond *beyond*." She waved a fork and sent potato flying to indicate the distance. "And you have the face to suggest that Basil's playing at it?"

Lady Colveden was baffled. "But it was you, Aunt Bray: you said in your letter that he played the trumpet."

"I said nothing of the kind. I said that Basil was a Trumpeter. It's wonderful. A Trumpeter's the highest office you can reach—except for a Serene. Beside the Master himself, of course. I," announced Aunt Bray, "am a Serene. That"—she dropped her knife and extended her hand—"is my badge to prove it." Upon the third finger was a white plastic ring. "Basil's is blue. And the Master himself wears yellow: his naturally is gold. The less ranks have other colors to distinguish them."

Nigel scooped potato from the carpet. "Like grading chickens?" he inquired.

"Nothing of the kind," she snapped. "It's simply that people must recognize one's rank. You can't expect Serenes to mingle with the lesser fry like Greenhorns."

"Greenhorns?" echoed Lady Colveden.

"Greenhorns," Aunt Bray explained, "are the beginners; they're green. Then come the Servers, they're red; then Majordomes, they're black; then blue for Trumpeters, and white for the Serenes. It's wonderful. You've no idea what it all means."

"Well, no, I haven't," admitted Lady Colveden. "But I expect it's all very satisfactory if you like that sort of thing."

"You're coming with me to the meeting at Maidstone and shall hear the Master himself. He's wonderful."

"Did you start as a Greenhorn?" Nigel asked.

"Certainly not," replied Aunt Bray. "But Basil did. The dear boy became so enthusiastic that I let him give a small donation, and then when they recognized his worth they moved him up."

Sir George was paying attention. "You give a small donation?"

For a moment Mrs. Trenthorne was thrown off balance, then she said quickly, "A trifle—a mere five thousand pounds. I could hardly have done less, considering they had made me a Serene. They recognized my subliminals, you see."

"What's this secret place?" he asked.

"Only the chosen few—" She stopped; her face flamed. "Secret? I don't know what you're talking about."

"In your letter."

"It was not. A secret? Really, George. A secret place?" she honked derisively. "I never mentioned such a thing. I wouldn't dream of it."

He let it ride. Didn't like the sound of it. Not the drill at all. Look into it.

Plummergen church was full; but not for prayer.

On Sunday the shops were closed; the church was then the easy place for villagers to congregate when gossiping was warm upon the tongue. The service over, they could meet outside, discuss the latest tidbit, destroy new characters, then strew the seared remains among the gravestones before returning home for well-earned roast and spuds.

This morning gossip was at boiling point and overspilled before its time, to ripple through the pews in murmurous buzz. The Reverend Arthur Treeves took to the pulpit, talked to air. His sermon for today was not inspired, which was just as well, since no one paid attention. Even his sister Molly, up in front, allowed her mind to wander. What were they up to now, with all this whispering? Thank heaven Arthur never noticed things till they were forced on him. But this was really quite disgraceful; she'd never known them to be so bad. Not even through the row when Mrs. Welsted, down with flu, refused to let Miss Pydell have the key for daily practice at the organ, with the result that poor Pydell now attended Rye, which made for awkwardness. She looked around, looked stern and shh'd. To no effect—or only for a space. She leaned back, closed her eyes and concentrated, trying to catch odd words, determined to gather if she could what all this chatter was about. She heard the words "Its eyes were starin'." Well, no villager who was worth his salt ever saw eyes that weren't. "She waved 'er brolly round and cursed the Nut, who come all over queer." Miss Nuttel feeling queer? A cold perhaps. "Poor little mite, she 'acked its 'ead off, 'ung it up and left it there to drip." Cut what off? They must be talking of Miss Seeton since they'd mentioned an umbrella. Poor Miss Seeton. Such an asset to the village. Couldn't these silly people ever learn to mind their own affairs? "Ought to be burn, she ought." What was this? "Good duckin's what she needs." "Flew straight out through the window on 'er brolly—they, saw it plain as plain." "Dangerous." "I'm keeping Eileen back from school, that's certain."

The sermon and Miss Treeves' patience ended. The service wound to its conclusion and they all trooped out to fill the graveyard with excited clack. A group of parents seethed in protest around the schoolmaster. Mr. Jessyp put his foot down hard and kept it there. Any parent whose child was absent from school without a medical certificate on Monday would be in trouble, he advised. Martha Bloomer held a raging court. To think that people could be that daft to think her bramble jelly was a baby. You wouldn't credit it. And as for those Nuts, she'd give 'em peeping toms, the prying cats. And as for Miss Nuttel's fainting, serve her right. Pity she ever came round, in her opinion. The Colvedens, without Aunt Bray, who'd stayed at home to nurse her new religion, learned of the latest rumors from Miss Treeves. Miss Nuttel and Mrs. Blaine maintained that Miss Seeton was boiling babies' heads for supper. Well, Meg Colveden had always thought, but now she knew, that both the Nuts were mad.

Dinnertime sent the villagers home split into two camps: which meant that everything was normal and the village was itself. Was, or was not, Miss Seeton a real witch? Some children said she wasn't; their parents swore she was. Some parents laughed the idea to scorn; *their* children had seen her, brolly-mounted, riding the night sky. The garage owner feared there might of course be something in it; the postmaster on the other hand saw nothing there to fear. The Reverend Arthur and Miss Treeves refuted the idea; the Welsteds from the draper's shop accepted it as true. Miss Nuttel and her friend insisted that they knew it for a fact; Lady Colveden said that fact only proved both them were fools.

There was only one person undisturbed. Miss Seeton did not know of the discussion, knew nothing of witchcraft—a subject which she might, perhaps, have felt was not, in common sense, a subject to discuss.

* * *

On Monday morning Miss Seeton looked down at the teacher's desk. There was a typed schedule for her guidance and a book, *General Mathematics*. Oh, dear. And she had so hoped ... But it couldn't be helped now. She sat down and faced the class. She smiled and said, "Good morning." They chorused back, "Good morning, miss," and appeared to settle down to work. Well, that was a good thing. So long as the children knew what to do perhaps it wouldn't be so bad. She looked at the book again. At the bottom of the cover it said "With Answers." Thank goodness for that. She checked the schedule, opened the book and found the page to see what they were at. Mutterings and sniggerings had been growing at the desks. The leader of the class, a wag, held up his hand.

"Please, miss. You gonna teach us t' fly?" They waited, thrilled, expectant: that should finish her.

Miss Seeton raised her head in mild surprise. She studied them. Wishful Peter Pans? No, with the modern boy it would be space ships, she supposed, jet airplanes. And for the girls, one imagined, air hostess. "I'm afraid I have no pilot's license," she regretted.

A shout of laughter greeted this riposte. A real comic. Bang on with the snappy answers. Need to watch your step with this one. Quick as you please and real sarky with it.

Miss Seeton examined the questions. *Express each of the following ratios as simply as possible in the form a : b. Q.13. 12cm: 4cm.* She turned to *Answers.* Yes, here it was. *13.3.1.* Miss Seeton frowned, reread the question. *3 : 1?* Then what had happened to the *a* and *b?* And where were *c* and *m?* Really, it was very worrying. Perhaps, she hoped, the children knew. She glanced down the page. Two headings met her eye. *Taxation.* For eleven-year-olds? Good gracious. And *Rates.* Oh, dear. But these were just the problems that were worrying her. She took a piece of paper and began to note things down. Q.9 was *House rent £60 with tax at £18.* It seemed extremely cheap. But then, of course, she hadn't rent. But had she house tax? What was house tax anyway? She certainly had rates. She looked again. It didn't mention rates. Was house tax rates, or were rates house tax? *Q.8* said *Income £1000 tax £400.* Well, yes. But if your income was *£400,* what then? It didn't say. She wrote again. A voice piped up.

"Please, miss. This income tax. If that's as much as what it is and then there's all these other taxes on sweets, tobacco and the rest, it seems to me they're taking more than what you've got."

Miss Seeton studied what she'd written. It seemed so to her too. "Well," she said at last, "I must admit it looks that way. Let's try and work it out. Supposing someone had so much for income but no rent—though rates, of course—and then there's tax and all these other things… ." They questioned her. They needed facts and figures.

"Miss, would this someone need football boots?" she was asked.

Well, no. She didn't think they would.

"And sweets—does she eat a lot of them?" Well, no, not many. Very few, in fact. That was good: and what about … They got to work. They left their places, walked around, plied her with questions, discussed the answers and made lists. The girls took food, clothes, linen and the like. The boys took capital, expenditure and tax; allowed for holidays and help.

While they were thus engrossed, Miss Seeton's eyes strayed to the next page in the book. It was headed *Bankruptcy*. She sighed. The bell rang. She stood up. There were protests. "Wait, miss." "Hang on, miss." "Just a tick, miss, we're nearly there." "Please, miss, we 'aven't finished." There was a final flurry; comparing notes, assessing this, resolving that. Miss Seeton sat and waited. The leader of the class, his waggery forgotten, jumped up with pride.

"We've done it, if you please, miss, we got the answer," he announced. "You'll 'ave to take a job."

* * *

The late-afternoon sun sinking red behind; gulls wheeling over the sea; dry grass on sand bent before the wind, stained scarlet by the dying sun, shadowed in rags by streaking cloud. Shadowed rags streaming across a yellowing sky, scurrying thwart blood-tinted earth.

So very dramatic. But so difficult to catch the color. And so much more difficult to capture movement. Miss Seeton laid down her brush. Though, one must admit, one did hope that it would not be quite so windy with the children here. It always involved so much chasing after paper. It really was very kind of Lady Colveden to take the trouble to bring her. Of course, as one of the school governors, Lady Colveden had known of the proposed children's outing, but to drive one out here in order to choose the view and get the preparatory work done, especially since one understood that she had a guest staying in the house ... Miss Seeton looked at her watch. The two hours were nearly up and Lady Colveden would be back at any moment. She began to pack her things. She put her finger to the paper. No, the sketch was not quite dry. She'd leave that till the last.

Hearing footsteps on the grass, Miss Seeton turned with a smile to say that she was ready. Oh. But how quite lovely. Words failed one. One didn't know how to express it. Miss Seeton didn't try; she stood and stared. The girl smiled.

"Hello. Sorry if I'm interrupting. Don't mind me, I won't bother you. I just got out of the car to stretch my legs and look around. I'm on my way to some little one-horse village called Plummergen. Going to put up at the local pub and thought I'd have a look at the district first." She took a gold cigarette case from her bag and proffered it. Wordless still, Miss Seeton shook her head. The girl lit a cigarette, dragged deep and let smoke run from her nostrils. "Painting the local beauty spots? Wish I had talent." She laughed. "There are a few things I could …" She saw Miss Seeton's effort. The laughter died. She gave Miss Seeton a strange look; abruptly she swung around and walked away.

Slowly Miss Seeton folded over her sketching frame, gathered her paraphernalia and moved toward the road. She was rather silent on the return journey with Lady Colveden. She refused an invitation to tea, somewhat to Meg Colveden's relief since she could not imagine Miss Seeton and Aunt Bray hitting it off. Miss Seeton, it appeared, had a previous engagement. That huge young sergeant from Scotland Yard had come down on holiday and was staying at the George and Dragon and he and Anne Knight had telephoned Miss Seeton and asked themselves to tea.

At the beginning of the tea party, despite a cheerful log fire, now that the days were drawing in, there was some constraint. Miss Seeton was a little embarrassed. For her, Sir Hubert Everleigh's letter hung like a gray cloud over the proceedings. For the sergeant, who had been issued with a copy of the document, it loomed like a black pall. It was all very well for the Oracle to say, I don't want to write myself, Bob, or interfere unless I have to—as the A.C.'s written in person it would be tactless—but I'll lay you five to one she refuses; she won't understand what's wanted of her and she'll dream up at least a dozen reasons against it, so it's for you to knock them down and make her agree. But how did you make someone agree to something that they didn't want to do; especially if that something was something quite unsuitable and something that they shouldn't've been asked to do anyway? Why couldn't they have left things as they were? After all, they could always've asked her to do the odd drawing, like they'd done before. But the A.C.'d cracked down on that. He'd said they'd no right to ask an outsider to take risks they weren't paid for. But no one'd ever asked Miss Seeton to take risks. She—well, she just took 'em without knowing. Also the A.C.'d said that judging by what'd gone on in the other two cases she'd got mixed up in, it'd be cheaper to have her officially attached to the force in the long run anyway. And old Brimstone at Ashford hadn't made things any easier by ringing him up as soon as he'd got down here, telling him to get cracking because she was wanted for this Nuscience meeting at Maidstone, but he couldn't ask her as things stood now till she was signed up. Signed up? He had a pocketful of forms he was supposed to get her to sign. But how the devil were you supposed to get someone to sign something they didn't want to sign, especially when that something was something … Oh, hell.

Anne had been asking how Miss Seeton had fared at the school, since she had been intrigued to hear that many of the children had developed a sudden and surprising interest in finance and would seem to be a collection of budding accountants. She noticed her hostess' growing discomfiture and broke off. She looked at them both. She put down her plate and chuckled.

"Listen," she suggested. "I know it's not my business but wouldn't it be better if you two got it over with and then we could enjoy ourselves? Bob's so scared you're going to say no, he hardly dares open his mouth in case he brings the subject up by mistake. And from the look of it"—she gave Miss Seeton a sympathetic smile—"well, you aren't exactly happy about it either. But we can't all sit round and go on pretending that assistant commissioners don't exist, because they do. Can't we"—she appealed to them both—"sort of agree that it's a good idea, or a bad idea, and then forget it?" Miss Seeton grew pink; Bob red. There was a silence. Anne shook her head in mock despair. "Well, anyway," she said, "could I have another cup of tea and some more cake?"

Miss Seeton laughed, apologized and attended to her duties. "You're quite right, Anne." She passed the cake to Bob. "I'm being silly. You see, really, though I suppose I should have, I couldn't imagine that it was, in fact, meant to be serious." Bob was comforted: that put old Sir Heavily in his place; she'd thought he was funning.

"That's lese majesty," Anne told her. "Even I'm learning that you have to take the assistant commissioner seriously."

"Of course." Miss Seeton was dubious. It was … so diffi-cult to express. Although she realized, perfectly, that drawing would be her main requirement, one did also know that anyone connected with the police must be prepared, at all times, to undertake any other job that might arise. Like the Scouts. And, of course, the Guides. Being prepared, she meant. "It's just that it's so—unusual. After all, at my age, not that one would mind the uniform exactly—should that ever become necessary—but to join the police force"—her troubled earnestness was almost too much for Anne—"when one doesn't even understand traffic and things of that kind; you do see that one can't—without the training, that is to say. So I thought that—well, in a way, it must be one. A joke, I mean."

Bob spluttered. The black pall had lifted. Traffic. He choked on cake crumbs. Miss Seeton in a uniform at Hyde Park corner or at Marble Arch directing traffic with a wave of her umbrella. "Oh, please," he gasped, "I wish you would," and went into another paroxysm. That would do it. That would solve the problem. All London's traffic stationary for miles and miles. And miles. Right into the suburbs. Never to move again. He hadn't felt so happy in a year.

Gradually, between convulsions, they sorted the thing out. The suggestion was, it was explained, that Miss Seeton should receive a small retainer and that in return the Yard should have the first call on her services; to send her anywhere they wished, expenses paid, to see people, to make drawings upon request and each time she was called in she would be paid pro rata for the job. In her mind a fresh young voice repeated, "Miss, you'll 'ave to take a job."

And so Miss Seeton signed, filled in, initialed, read *Whereas* and *In the event of* and *This contract to be renewed annually and revised if necessary by mutual agreement*, and signed the papers Bob produced.

Chapter 5

"Today I'm going to talk to you of Freedom."

The hall at Maidstone was packed. Miss Seeton sat forward, intent with concentration. On this, her first official assignment for the police, she must really do her best. Such a very pleasant boy who'd brought her here. And colorful, in that pink sweater with the turned-down collar—roll neck, she believed—and then the jacket in a near-magenta. Not, in truth, perhaps, the happiest combination. But colorful. One had somehow thought of the police as being cropped. But no. This Mr. Foxon's hair was long—well, quite—and wavy. She'd brought a note pad to make notes; record impressions. She made a note; recorded an impression. *Freedom;* inscribed Miss Seeton.

"Freedom," continued the speaker, "which means freedom of the senses …"

"Poppycock," muttered Sir George in the front row. Aunt Bray looked outraged. Lady Colveden signed to her husband to keep quiet.

"… freedom of the mind, freedom of the spirit and freedom of expression …"

The majority of the audience sat enrapt, but to Bob, who had slipped in at the back with Anne, it sounded gibblegabble.

"… freedom," emphasized the lecturer, "from sin; freedom to love."

"Bosh," grunted Sir George.

Rather a lot of freedom, wrote Miss Seeton.

Nigel, who had accompanied his parents at his father's asking, was half turned in his seat. That girl: that gold hair; those red lights in it. That girl: those eyes; that mouth. That … girl. He also sat enrapt. The only words of all the carefully worked up rodomontade that got through to him were "freedom to love."

"Here in the Western world," went on the orator, "we are bound like Prometheus of old by chains; chains whose links are forged—forged," he repeated, "by false concepts, forged by material considerations, by fear and by wrong thinking. Far in the East in ashrams, in solitary cells, in lonely monasteries, the yogis have known the answers to these problems for countless centuries. This world does not exist. Ah"—he paused and looked around the auditorium—"that surprises you. And yet I tell you that it's true. You think in material terms of different substances; but once you can free your mind from this illusion and attain pure knowledge, or chit …"

Miss Seeton frowned, uncertain. These foreign languages. So difficult to spell.

"… you'll find that there is but one illusion—the Great Illusion—which is the world, ourselves and all about us; all nothing but the mere reflection of God the Divine Creator. Maya, the principle of illusion which denies reality, or om. Once you have achieved maya you can attain true worship; worshiping all illusion as a reflection of God." For a moment he stood staring into space. Then: "Eternal life. Eternal …" he reiterated slowly. "Never to die. The Western dream: the

Eastern reality. For never doubt it is reality; a reality within the grasp of all possessing faith and perseverance. You might ask, What has this to do with freedom? My answer is, Mukti."

"Hear, hear," agreed Sir George, who shared with Miss Seeton an inability to grasp the finer points of Sanskrit.

"Mukti," explained the speaker, "means liberation from the wheel of birth and death; a soul in freedom. It is a state that any human being can achieve—it has been achieved by many in the East. Among the mystics there I have talked and worked with men older than the centuries; men who know your thoughts and actions before you can formulate them for yourself. Some of you may smile, but this is scientific fact. There is much that I am not allowed to tell you, but this I have been permitted: to bring to the West the essential teachings in a shortened version—in Nuscience—almost you might call it a shortcut to Eternal Truth. I have also, at my special pleading, been granted permission to reveal to those few whose subliminals I can recognize the actual Secret of Eternal Life. For some of us"—he shook his head in whimsical reproof—"the fleshly desires, the carnal appetites, make maya difficult. But this is but another facet of the fear I spoke of—and I have told you not to be afraid. Remember that many of the saints led far from blameless lives before they fulfilled their purpose. Do not fear sin. Sin is man's base inheritance through which he must be redeemed. Unless you truly understand the nature of sin there can be no salvation. Don't be afraid of sinful thoughts or acts, for without them how shall you be purged? It is an old saying but a true one that without sin there can be no redemption. We look up"—he suited action to the word—"and see the ripe fruit high above us, but we cannot reach the fruit because we are weighed down by chains. My friends"—he flung his arms wide; a gold ring glittered on one hand—"throw off these chains. Rise up as free men and women to pluck the fruit which is your birthright. Do I say birthright?" he demanded.

Well, actually he had, allowed Miss Seeton.

"Did I say birthright?" he insisted.

Should one, perhaps, in kindness, tell him so?

"The world is a misconception in itself. We are not born," he told them. "We but return here for a span, a term, a moment merely. A term," he emphasized in an ominous tone, "a moment that is ending—that is all but gone." A shiver of apprehension ran through the hall. "For that," he warned them, "is the message that I bring you from Beyond. Life, as we understand it in the West with our puerile lack of imagination, our childish mental failure to grasp the Infinite, is over." There were gasps of fear; he rode the wave. "Done with," he urged; a prophet of old with a denunciatory hand held high and menacing; a modern Jove with thunderbolt upraised. "This earth has run its course." The vibrant prophecy seemed to dim the lights, casting an eerie shadow. "Those of you who have read my book *Beyond the Beyond*, published by the Offset Press at thirty shillings ..."

Beyond the Beyond—Offset at 30/-, dutifully noted Miss Seeton.

"... will realize something of what I mean—will appreciate the awful significance of what is come to pass. For make no mistake: our time, both yours and mine, the time of all of us, is now upon us." Some of the more emotional of his audience, already indoctrinated by previous inoculations, were in tears. Miss Nuttel held her breath. Her friend expelled hers in a sob. An elderly gentleman in the fourth row blew his nose. "But don't despair," their mentor encouraged them, "for that is the reason I am here today. I come to save you. Do you know how to breathe?" he asked them sternly. His hearers looked surprised, a little sheepish. "Breath is the source of life," he informed them. The inspired truth came as a revelation. "By proper breathing—by pranayama— we control our destinies, our movements; control not only the movement of our spirits, but of our bodies too. You think man cannot fly: I tell you that he can. Governments throw your money into spaceships, nuclear rockets for a brief journey to the moon, and in doing so destroy the stratosphere. Our weather's gone, our health is ruined and now our world itself must die, destroyed by man's ineptitude. But I have knowledge that transcends these petty sciences. Nuscience can fly you to the stars—each one of you—with no motor but the mind."

In a room behind the speaker's platform a young man wearing a single earphone sat with his fingers—the third of the right hand sported a blue plastic ring—on the controls of a high-fidelity tape recorder. The door opened and two men entered.

"How's the old goat doing, Basil?" the shorter, squarer of the two men asked. "Sticking to his script?"

"Not bad, Duke," Basil Trenthorne replied. "I took the Mastermind's cold tea away from him before the meeting"—he waved at a pocket brandy flask which lay beside the recorder— "and said that was it till he'd spoken his little piece." He listened a moment. "Just coming up to the breathing," he told them. "He's buzzing around the stars at the moment on his motormind. The breathing always gets 'em if they do it hard enough. Gets 'em giddy enough to think they're going places. Always good for a few converts."

The mouth of the man he had called Duke twisted. "Helps to keep the regulars forking out too."

The speaker on the platform poured water from a glass jug on the table beside him. He sipped. Once more he faced the hall. "The first essential is to learn to breathe." He pressed a forefinger against one nostril. "You take a deep inhalation—puraka. Then hold the breath for as long as possible. Then"—he dropped his arm and placed the forefinger of the other hand against his other nostril—"from the other side you expel—rechaka—every trace of breath in the body. Practice this," he exhorted them, "as often as you can. Pranayama is but the first step—the first vital step—to complete control. Through the ages the greatest men have done it. The great teachers of the Old Testament did it. Our Lord, the greatest yogi of them all, did it. I can do it. And," he assured them, "you too can do it."

" 'The Dutch in old Amsterdam do it,/Not to mention the Finns,' " bubbled Anne in Bob Ranger's ear.

Many in the audience were indeed trying to do it. Stertorous breathing whistled and snorted round the hall. To the uninstructed eye the assembly resembled an insubordinate class thumbing their noses at the headmaster. *Practices Yoga* jotted down Miss Seeton, *without sufficient knowledge. Most unwise.* Several of the neophytes were beginning to feel peculiar. Miss Nuttel, who had expelled her breath so hard she could regain none, tilted sideways and Mrs. Blaine produced smelling salts.

While the congregation practiced for their first flight of fancy, Miss Seeton's attention wandered. Those twisted turbans.

So very difficult to wear. And even on white hair that shade of red entwined with yellow and puce was not becoming. It must be, one supposed, the Colvedens' relative since she was sitting with them. Nigel was next to his mother, but turned away. He seemed intent on something else. Oh. No wonder. There was that quite lovely girl who had spoken to her yesterday by the sea.

While Miss Seeton looked around, from his aisle seat Foxon watched her. This was a ruddy odd stint and no mistake. Bring this old trout to this crazy meeting, look after her and keep an eye on her reactions. The chief inspector must've lost the north. Of course, old Brimmers was old, but this caper—he must be getting senile, lost his grip. As for reactions—well, she'd made a note or two. He leaned a little, reading them. Didn't mean a thing; could've done better himself. And now she was getting bored and had started doodling. Portrait of the speaker? Might come in useful, he supposed. He watched as with quick deft strokes a goat's head appeared upon the paper. No, she'd chucked her hand in— who could blame her?—and was drawing farmyard animals. The goat, in three-quarter view, had a wicked eye; it leered. A touch or two and a white wing appeared in the dark hair above the ear. A finger was sketched in against one nostril. The speaker as a billy goat—well, give her best. Caught off guard, he gave a bay of laughter. Within seconds he felt a tap upon his shoulder. A young man wearing a black plastic ring was standing by him.

"Excuse me, sir," the young man said, "but we don't want any of that. It disturbs people's concentration. So if you wouldn't mind leaving, sir ..."

"Well, I would," said Foxon, and sank lower in his seat.

The young man put his hand upon Foxon's arm above the elbow; pinched a nerve. The pain brought Foxon gasping to his feet.Another young man, also black-ringed, took his other arm. Between them they walked him up the aisle. Foxon began to struggle. They pulled his jacket down, pinioning his arms: his wallet fell to the floor. A third young man retrieved the case, flicked through it and, holding it out, followed in their wake. Bob half rose and then sat back. Better not interfere. The Oracle would have his hide if he started mixing in it without permission. That was Foxon of the Ashford C.I.D.; he'd recognized him. What did the silly twit want to go sounding off like that for? And come to that, why hadn't he put up a fight? Pretty good scrapper, Foxon, he remembered. And all these young men springing up from nowhere ... Slickly done; hardly a soul had noticed. Professional. The one who'd got Foxon's wallet would've tabbed him—neat job. Foxon'd cop it when he got back to his Div. H.Q. He cast a casual but appraising glance around the hall. Yes—when you came to look, there were quite a few of them. This racket was off, all right; and bent. Good for old Brimstone. But that left Miss Seeton on her own. Should be all right, he supposed; still, better keep an eye out.

In the back room behind the platform a Majordome reported.

"Detective Constable Foxon of the Ashford Division, sir," he told the man called Duke. "Sitting next to an old geezer with a notebook. Created a disturbance. We ran him out, dusted him down and apologized, but told him he'd have to wait for his friend outside."

"This geezer with the notebook?"

"Elderly party, female, sir. Looks harmless."

"Right," said the man called Duke. He looked a question at his taller companion, who nodded. "But for safety get her notebook when the meeting breaks up. No rough stuff; just something casual. But get it and find out who she is."

"Will do, sir." The young man saluted and withdrew.

Poor Mr. Foxon. Miss Seeton was curious. What had happened to him? He'd made a funny noise and then a young man had spoken to him, and then he'd jumped up without a word and gone. Probably something urgent to do with the police. But how, she began to speculate, would she get home? She put her notebook into her bag and closed it. Really, one had done one's best. Had tried to pay attention. But the whole thing seemed—well, a little childish. In fact, frankly, silly. Naturally one realized, of course, that it was essential for the police to investigate any new movement or religion—if one could call it that—just in case. And how truly considerate it was of them to send someone like oneself, who would be in no way remarkable in such a gathering, nor cause the promoters of the meeting any embarrassment. At all events it was now perfectly clear that there was nothing in this Nuscience that need disturb the authorities. As for Mr. Brinton's suggestion that she should follow it up and say that she wished to become a member herself ... One realized now that it had not, of course, been meant seriously, but was just an example of Mr. Brinton's what-used-to-be-described-as rather pawky sense of humor. Miss Seeton smiled in belated recognition of the chief inspector's jest. She concentrated again on the platform. The lecturer was, one supposed, impressive. Tall, and with that profile, with the dark hair with those white side wings, he reminded one a little of an actor. But to advocate that yoga breathing exercise which, one feared, he didn't quite understand—so very rash. It could do harm. Of course she did not pretend to be an expert, only a beginner, and, of course, had never read those chapters at the end about the mind, in that most helpful book *Yoga and Younger Every Day*, but one did know enough to know that any exercise done too hard at first and without the proper practice could be injurious. And now he was talking about astronomy, saying that everyone—well, actually he called it one's soul, or life force, whatever that might mean—came from other planets. Saturn and Venus he'd spoken of, though she couldn't be quite sure that he hadn't mentioned others, guarded by monks and nuns of different colors. And that one came from there and could go back to there at will. He said that he'd been back there several times. Back, that was, to whichever one of them it was he favored. But really the whole thing seemed a little muddled. Because if life on these planets was so very satisfactory, so well organized, then one failed to grasp, or failed to grasp entirely, quite why, in that case, people ever left. The planets, she meant.

A young man slid into the seat beside her. "Your friend," he whispered, "wasn't very well. He said he'd wait for you outside."

Miss Seeton thanked him. Poor Mr. Foxon. Then it wasn't police business after all. Would he be well enough to drive her home? she wondered. If not, he would make some arrangement, she felt sure. She settled back in her seat prepared once more to listen.

One of 'em had slipped into the vacant seat next to Miss Seeton—not so good. Bob turned to Anne and whispered.

The peroration from the platform was drawing to a close.

"I do not," proclaimed the lecturer, "ask that you should join us, I do not beg of you to join us, I can only implore you to save yourselves, to join us and be free. As Another once offered you salvation so do I now: that we true believers in the Christian Faith and in Nuscience shall have the grace to lead you from this present twilight of man's retrogression forward to liberation and the redemption of mankind. Amen."

After a moment of reverent silence the audience broke into tumultuous applause. Miss Seeton thought she would slip out quickly and see how Mr. Foxon was. But the young man in the aisle seat was clapping hard, seemed so enthusiastic, that one didn't like to say excuse me, or step over him, for fear of being rude. Finally the speaker took his last bow and retired. The audience rose and surged toward the exits. Miss Seeton reached the aisle and joined the stream heading for the main doors at the rear. Someone stumbled against her from behind; caught the strap of her bag in falling. Miss Seeton, pulled off balance, was twisted around and, throwing out her arm to save herself, brought the handle of her umbrella down with a crack on a young man's nose. He yelped, tears started from his eyes and he let go his hold.

"Oh, dear," apologized Miss Seeton. "Oh, dear, I am so sorry. Please forgive me. I do hope I haven't hurt you." She had no time for more: she was swept on with the crowd. Really, one hadn't realized that there were so many young people at the meeting. All around her there seemed to be young men. Quite three or four. She was jostled and again she felt a pull upon her bag. It was so very difficult, in such a crush. She would hang her bag upon her other arm for safety. She was shifting her grip upon her umbrella for the changeover, when she was bumped from the other side. Like a spear the umbrella's ferrule was driven into the young man on her left amidships. He gave a cry of pain, released her bag and doubled up.

"Oh, please, I am so dreadfully sorry. I was pushed," called out Miss Seeton. Really, with all this jostling there'd be an accident.

"Hello, Aunt Em," boomed a loud voice.

The three young men still left around Miss Seeton turned and stared. A beaming giant was bearing down on them. They hung back irresolute. A plain little girl with a humorous face ran forward.

"Aunt Em," gushed Anne. She threw her arms around Miss Seeton and kissed her. "Call him Bob," she whispered. "How lovely to see you," she enthused. "We thought we saw you from the back. We'd just slipped in. We'd never been to any of these meetings, and aren't they wonderful! We were so surprised to see you here, but then it's the sort of thing you've always found so interesting, isn't it? The speaker was magnificent, I thought, didn't you?"

Bob reached them, bent low and kissed Miss Seeton's cheek. She blushed. "Play up," he murmured in her ear.

Play? Up? Of course. But play at what? She wondered. She tried. They'd called her Aunt, and so ... She smiled. "Dear—er—Bob, and Anne." She patted the girl's hand. "What a pleasant surprise. And how are the children?" asked Miss Seeton brightly.

It was Bob's turn to blush. Anne laughed. It was really very naughty of Miss Seeton to give them more than one before they'd married. Sir George Colveden joined them.

"Hello, sir," said Bob quickly. "You've met my aunt, I think? Aunt Em," he added by way of explanation. "And Anne of course you know."

"Course." Sir George nodded; shook hands. "Good to see you." His aunt? He'd thought things were getting out of line back here. Couldn't make a proper recce—all those damn people—and in spite o' shoving couldn't get here quicker. Sir George addressed Miss Seeton. "Spotted you when we came in. Wondered if you'd like a lift home?" "How very kind of you, Sir George. So very thoughtful. But it's quite unnecessary. You see, I came with—"

"Us," cut in Bob. "Jolly good of you, sir," he exuberated, "but we'll run Aunt Em home. You see, with Anne being so tiny we've got lots of room." He thought of them squashed into Anne's small car and hoped he'd be forgiven.

The three young men who had stood aside, observing, listening, followed them to the main entrance, listening still; observed Foxon's reaction as he stood by a table at which a girl with a stack of pamphlets, forms and books in front of her was selling copies of *Beyond the Beyond* and handing out red rubber balloons in the shape of space men. They observed Miss Seeton's hesitation when she saw Foxon; observed Bob's bustling of her through the doors. Standing outside, they observed the departure in Anne's car; observed Sir George leave with his wife and son and Mrs. Trenthorne and, later, observed Foxon, disconsolate, drive off in solitary state at the wheel of a large dark sedan with double driving mirrors and a tall antenna.

Chapter 6

Superintendent Delphick lounged, Sergeant Ranger sat and Detective Constable Foxon stood in Chief Inspector Brinton's office.

Brinton glared at his subordinate. "All right, you've had time to think up six good reasons why you mucked it up. Let's have 'em."

Red in the face, Foxon answered, "No excuse, sir."

Brinton humphed. "That's a change. So all right, let's have it in your own words what happened. And," he warned as Foxon opened his mouth, "not in the official jargon. None of your 'I was proceeding' stuff. Stretch your invention and try and imagine you're a human being; then tell it."

Foxon did. Nothing had happened, he reported, until he'd laughed. Even then, nothing that couldn't've been explained away. In fact they had explained it afterward: said they were very sorry, but laughing out loud at one of their meetings was like someone laughing in church, and they couldn't have that, it upset the congregation—that was what they'd called the audience—insisted they were sure he hadn't understood and hoped there were no ill feelings. Beautiful manners they'd had, commented Foxon—afterward. Then they'd asked him if he'd mind waiting for his friend outside in the lobby. As for the rest, at the beginning there'd only been this old chap on the platform spouting a lot of hogwash.... He stumbled. "That is, I mean, sir, it was—"

"Hogwash," agreed Brinton.

Foxon gained confidence. "Well, sir, there he was standing up spouting a lot of tripe and onions and Miss Seeton was taking the odd note. I took a squint but they didn't seem to mean anything—till she did the drawing. And then suddenly the notes were awfully funny too."

"No need to go into that," said Brinton. "We've got her notebook here."

"Hang on." Delphick sat forward. "This drawing—I've seen it, of course, but tell me, how exactly did she do it?"

Foxon turned, surprised. "Funny you should mention that, sir. She didn't, if you know what I mean." Delphick nodded encouragement. "What I mean is, the old buffer on the platform had got 'em all started on some breathing caper and—well, she seemed to get bored and started looking around. Then suddenly, before you could blink, she was doodling. Not seeming to pay attention, if you know what I mean; rather like those cartoonists you get sometimes on piers. Didn't mean a thing to me at first—just a goat. Then"—he sketched two quick strokes in the air—"then all of a sudden it was the old guy speaking, and what with that and what she'd written—well, I'm afraid it was too much for me, sir."

Delphick nodded again with satisfaction. Brinton grunted, reviewed Miss Seeton's sketch, which lay upon his desk, and acknowledged, "Probably'd have been too much for me."

"Then," resumed Foxon, "one of these types touched me on the shoulder and told me to scarper. I said I wouldn't.

He caught my arm just above here"—he indicated—"and pressed. I don't know exactly what he did—must've been a nerve, I suppose. The world blew up and I couldn't even speak. Then two of 'em frog-marched me out. I did try to have a whack at them but they pulled the old jacket trick; there was nothing to do except yell murder, which"—he looked at his chief with apology—"I didn't think you'd want, sir."

"Didn't," conceded Brinton. He stared at Foxon a moment. "So all right, for pity's sake sit down, boy. If you go on thinking you're on the mat and go on shuffling your feet you'll wear the damn thing out." He eyed with disfavor the hessian cord which did duty for a carpet. Thankfully Foxon subsided onto an upright chair against the wall.

Delphick leaned over and took Miss Seeton's notebook off the desk. He studied the drawing. "Is this a good likeness of the lecturer?"

"Well—no," admitted Foxon. "Not like, sir, but it's him all right and the way he looked, dead to a T—'cept that she made him funny," he added as an afterthought.

Delphick produced a photograph, a copy of a studio portrait, and made comparison. "Certainly the likeness doesn't show. I wonder if there could be some other meaning behind this goat business?"

"No." Brinton was positive. "The old girl saw him as a silly goat—which from all accounts he is—and so all right, she put down what she saw."

Put down what she saw.... Delphick mused. A newspaperwoman, Mel Forby, had once pointed out to him that in the ordinary way, as an artist, Miss Seeton was painstaking, accurate and bad, but when she sometimes, unconsciously, allowed her hand to rule her head she could be brilliant.

Brilliant in intuition as well as draftsmanship. He shelved it for the moment and addressed his sergeant.

"What did you make of it, Bob, from what you saw?"

"Not a lot, sir; except to agree with Foxon, they're professionals. The way they jacketed him and knocked his wallet out, and then the one behind picked it up and had a quick flip through before he gave it back, was slick—as neat a job as you'd want to see. The way they did the whole thing was professional, sir. I'd say very few people noticed he'd gone, and I'd swear nobody'd noticed they'd chucked him out. But there were a lot of them about—the young toughs—dotted round the hall. Oh, yes," he remembered, "and they all wore black bands, third finger of the right hand, and—well, that's really all, sir."

"All?" echoed Delphick innocently. "I understood you went in for amateur dramatics at the end."

Bob crimsoned. "Well, sir, it was all getting a bit—er—off, sir. I didn't like it when one of the hoodlums took the seat next to Miss Seeton, but afterward they started crowding her and it didn't look so good. It was a bit difficult looking over the tops of people, but as far as I could see she turned round and bashed one of them in the face with her umbrella, then upped and gave another one of them a jab in the—well, she got him nicely, sir. With her umbrella, of course," he clarified hastily. "And one way and another it seemed time for butting in."

Delphick, who had heard the story from Sir George, kept his face straight. "And so you adopted her as family. Or is she, after all, your dear Aunt Em, and you've been holding out on me?"

"Yes, sir. I—er—mean no, sir. I mean, yes, I did but I mean, no, she isn't, sir."

"Your meaning," Delphick assured him, "is crystal clear. And how did Miss Seeton take this rigmarole?"

"Oh, very well, sir." And all at once Bob's discomposure left him. There was something in it, come to that. After all, the Oracle himself had told him once that Miss Seeton was a sort of universal aunt. And in the car on the way back, with Anne still calling her Aunt and laughing, and Miss Seeton herself not minding, or not seeming to, and him thinking of her in that way too, she was somehow easier to cope with. He didn't mean she wasn't off. She was. And half the things she did were off-er still. But lots of people had eccentric aunts, and as an aunt it was easier to—well, cope. A pity that she'd joined the Force—that was right off. But, in a way, aunt-wise, she seemed different, more— more likely somehow. Yes, he decided, he'd settle for her as an aunt.

The superintendent broke in on these reflections. "Did these young men stick around when you were all playing Happy Families?"

"Yes, sir, they did. And they were standing on the steps outside when we drove off."

Delphick frowned. "So your cover's blown as well as Foxon's, but, more important, it's blown Miss Seeton's too. You told me you thought it was her handbag they were after?"

"I think so, sir. In the car, she seemed to think it was people pushing accidentally, but she did say that twice she nearly lost her bag."

"Probably wanted to see her notes."

"Fat lot of good they'd've done them," remarked Brinton.

"But they aren't to know that," Delphick pointed out.

"We'll need to keep a watch where she's concerned. They appear to be a tough crew by all accounts—manners or no." He put Miss Seeton's sketch back on the desk.

Brinton glanced at it. "Oh, yes, by the way, what's all this yoga breathing stuff? What's she know about it?" Delphick interpreted. Miss Seeton, sometime previously, had taken up yoga exercises of which she had read in an advertise- ment to correct a certain stiffness in the joints. "You mean," demanded Brinton, "stands on her head? That sort of thing? No wonder she does half the things she does—it's softening of the brain."

"I've got a little on Nuscience, not much." Delphick threw over the photograph. "That's the man they call the Master; I had a few copies run off. Name's Hilary Evelyn, age forty-six, small-time actor; hasn't worked in the theater for the last two years; no private means as far as we can check, but seems flush, so presumably Nuscience pays him well. In the opinion of his late colleagues, a good actor but unreliable through drink; no brains whatever; also a womanizer. I imagine he's employed only as a figurehead. He might prove a weak link. Can't get a line on who's behind Nuscience. Everybody very cagey. Only name we've picked up is Duke, or *the* Duke—don't know which, or who he is. The other time Nuscience came to police notice was in Scotland about two years ago, in the Trossachs north of Glasgow. A lot of rumors; about the end of the world. Two or three hundred people trooped down to some cave to sit it out. When they finally came up again there was a complaint that they'd been robbed. The complaint was withdrawn—or rather the man died and his wife said it was all a mistake. The Glasgow boys investigated but couldn't prove it wasn't suicide. He'd threatened to kill himself several times—again only the wife's evidence—and that's how it was left; with a very fishy smell. I asked Glasgow to let me have anything they've got on file and also any details or rumors that anyone remembers. I had a chat with Sir George Colveden, who's worried about some distant cousin of his, a Mrs. Trenthorne, whom they all call Aunt Bray. Her son, Basil—Sir George won't have him in the house—got her interested in Nuscience: she coughed up the cash for the boy to become a Greenhorn and then bought herself in as a Serene, which according to Sir George is the misnomer of the century. Her Serenity cost her a cool five thousand pounds—it's incredible what people will fall for when it comes to insuring their immortal souls. The son was then upped to Trumpeter—God save us, the names they give themselves—presumably as a reward for bringing in his mum. I've checked on Master Basil and he's one of our little boys: twenty and done everything crooked he could dream up since he escaped from his pram. His ma's been buying him out of trouble from the age of ten and he completed his education in an approved school. Sir George thinks little Basil's helping them milk mama for all they, and he, can get. Apparently she let slip something about a Secret Place, but clammed up and denied it when questioned. The Colvedens and their Aunt Bray had a set-to after the Maidstone do and she's taken off to an hotel in Rye in a pet, though the son's still in Maidstone."

Brinton ruminated. "All right, so what it boils down to," he said at length, "is we thought they were crooked, now we know, but no proof of anything as usual. On the other hand, they know we're interested, which leaves them knowing more than us—as usual—and we'll just wait, as usual, till they step out of line. As we can't get Miss Seeton into

Nuscience now—though she certainly stirred things up and tipped us off about the bodyguards—here's something else"—he picked up a sheet of paper from his desk—"she might have a dekko at. Should be just her cuppa—things that go bump in the night. You told me once your Ass. Comm. thinks she's a catalyst for crime; so all right, me and Sir Hubert both. As she's stirred herself out of Nuscience, let's stick her back in witchcraft. Potter reports"—he waved the piece of paper—"Plummergen's got itself all of a twit. Some yobs've been seeing lights in the church at Iverhurst at night. Since the place isn't used and's falling to bits, it's given them the jitters. After the Malebury scare they see black magic everywhere. Might be something in it—it was in Iverhurst churchyard that Potter found his bits of burnt cow. He's had a look-see and found traces of another fire; and he thinks there's been goings on"—he glanced at the paper—"what he calls a potential occurrence—in the church itself. Could be a tramp, sightseers, lovers, or what have you, but Potter suggests we beat the wood. What's he think I've got? A private army? The wood's behind the church," he explained, "and comes right down to the grave-yard. Could put a couple of men on, I suppose, to keep watch, but they might be there for weeks and nothing happen. I'd rather get an idea if there's something to watch for first. Thought if we put Miss Seeton there one night—with her so full of ESP and all the rest of the alphabet—she might come up with a drawing or something that would give us a line. Anyway, now she's on the strength might just as well use her. At worst"—he tucked the paper back into a file and closed it—"maybe she'll start a fire of her own and burn the damn church down, which'd stop it."

Delphick was dubious. "You're asking a bit much, Chris; I don't suppose she knows anything about witchcraft."

"Then it's high time she learned," retorted Brinton. "According to Potter here"—he tapped the file—"half Plummergen's got her taped as the Witch of Endor. They've even dragged the postmaster into it; say he's running a witch's shop."

Delphick didn't like it. "ESP or no, Chris—and don't forget she wouldn't recognize extrasensory perception if she met it in the street—Miss Seeton's not a medium, she doesn't go into trance. I can't see what sort of drawing you'll get out of her, sitting there catching cold in an empty church. There'd be nothing for her to go on. Try getting her to sketch it by daylight—that might get something."

Brinton was stubborn. "No, Oracle, I want her there at night; get the feel of the place under the same conditions. I saw it by day when I was looking at bits of cow and it doesn't mean a thing, but at night I could see it being spooky." Delphick was unconvinced but yielded. After all, witchcraft was not his case. The chief inspector looked at Foxon. "You get yourself over to Plummergen and arrange with Miss Seeton to visit the church at night; make it early in the week."

Foxon stood up. "Yes, sir."

"And don't," he was told, "fall over your feet this time; don't knock the building down and don't have hysterics."

After Foxon's exit Delphick sat thoughtful. He had, as he had promised himself, been reading up on witchcraft; also he was alive to the circumstance that he was to a large extent instrumental in the launching of Miss Seeton on her new career and sensible of her aptitude for attracting turmoil. Something was nagging him. Miss Seeton's sketch. A goat? Why had she drawn a goat? Those quick, vital cartoons of hers so often bore a meaning of which she was unaware. Something about a goat ... Of course—witchcraft. Historically, from what he'd been reading on the subject, the goat had frequently been the symbol or disguise of the Devil. But then the goat, so far as he remembered, had been chiefly confined to France; certainly never in England. Still that wasn't to say that the more modern cults hadn't adopted it as an easy and effective disguise. Many of the better known paintings of sabbaths had included the goat. No ... perhaps it was a bit farfetched. In any case there was no connection with Nuscience. He got to his feet and began to pace the office. "What we need, Chris, to get anywhere with Nuscience is background. I thought of tackling Mrs. Trenthorne, but from what Sir George has told me she's a fool and bigoted, which means I'd get nowhere. She'd blab and all we'd've done would be to tip our hand. And I certainly can't see her son spilling any beans. There's big money behind Nuscience, which means we'll need gang warily. One thing that Glasgow did let slip was that they'd heard rumors of witchcraft and a coven meeting at about the time of the Nuscience complaint. Can there be a connection? And if so, how? Surely the two would be diametrically opposed. No use sending a man to Glasgow to do a bit of ferreting. Too long ago and all the trails are cold. The boys there will do a better job. It's their bailiwick and now that they've reason to poke around, although it's rather ancient history, I suppose it's barely possible they might come up with something. But that's what bugs me: background and history. History. I feel somehow the answer's there. I don't see how it's possible but"—he swung round on Brinton—"don't laugh—historically Miss Seeton's drawing of the goat could by a stretch of the imagination link up with witchcraft."

"Some stretch," observed Brinton.

"Right." Delphick was impatient. "I said it was reaching, but I've had more experience of the odd quirks in her sketches than you. I feel ... I feel somehow the answer should be there. If we could find some connection ... Could there be something somewhere in their history which would establish a link between witchcraft and Nuscience?"

Chapter 7

The link which the superintendent was seeking had been forged in Scotland some two years previously when two businessmen had met. Both men were ministers of religion: both had taken Christianity as a basis for their respective cults on the sound principle that since Christianity had proved reasonably successful it should give a firm foundation on which to adjust and improvise plus a ready-made audience willing to listen to negation or interpretation according to individual preference.

One man denied the Christian doctrine, reversed its teaching, derided Good and worshiped Evil, insisting that the True Faith sprang only from Below. The other professed to accept the Christian creed but expanded and improved upon it by preaching that the True Faith gravitated solely from Above; from the stars.

One glorified Sin as a way of life, the means to a paradise in Damnation after death. The other, more subtly, assuming sin to be inevitable, urged that without sin there could be no redemption and held that Celestial Happiness lay for all mankind upon the planet of his choice.

One, refuting Christianity, adopted a perverted form of an old, once happy, religion which through abuse and the denunciations of the early Christians has come to be known as Satanism. The other, embracing Christianity, adapted it to a new religion, Nuscience.

These two men, divergent in their approach, had two things in common, method and aim: to hoodwink the gullible; to make money.

By coincidence, or to be accurate, by the incidence of their professions, both men were nameless. Each in the course of years had used many aliases and names no longer had a meaning. One was of medium height and sturdy build and was inconspicuous and, fearing perhaps to lose his identity in his shifting world, was known as Duke. The other, tall, dark and saturnine, in his shiftless world had no permanent title. On one occasion when he had been checking a reference in the Book of Common Prayer a colleague had insisted on a name by which to call him. The tall man had turned to the confirmation service and from the restricted choice had chosen N. And N. he had remained.

Duke had selected Hell as his hunting ground. After studying the subject he had started witches' covens in various parts of the British Isles, attracting the seekers after pleasure and sensation by including the more lurid ceremonies, the more erotic details; but human sacrifice he frowned upon as unrewarding; murder, if at any time advisable, should only be done for his personal advantage. He insisted that all members at the meetings should be masked: the men to wear an animal's head of their choice and the women to be disguised by black face masks. It was a rule that whatever the members might take off during the ceremonies—and after a sabbath feast, in the course of the ensuing dance and orgy, they frequently took off everything—in no circumstances was the mask to be removed. It was explained to members on their initiation that the rule of the mask was for their own protection. No member could identify another and by the same token, in the event of trouble, no member could attempt the blackmail of another. Duke had decided from the start that the perquisite of blackmail must remain strictly his own. His physique was unimpressive for the role of Devil in these saturnalia, so to correct the impression he had chosen a long black shift and the Continental tradition of a goat's head. He prospered in a modest way, leaving each coven in the charge of a lieutenant or subdevil during his absences. The fees for membership were reasonable and the levy on those members who proved themselves worthy of blackmail was not extreme. Duke preferred the safety of an income derived in small sums from the many to the danger involved by demanding excessive amounts from the few. Each coven had its nucleus of thirteen and these with the subdevil as their leader were free to enroll as many followers as they wished, while taking reasonable precautions. The rules were few but strict. A convert renounced all erstwhile errors of faith, devoting body and soul to the Devil, who must be obeyed in all things. The vow itself was simple: one hand was placed upon the crown of the head, the other upon the sole of one foot, and all that lay between the two hands was dedicated to the service of the new Master. A covenant was signed. The covenants had been almost Duke's only outlay. He had had them ornamentally printed on parchment and they insisted, in old and misspelled English, on the candidate's free will and consent. Duke had felt, however, that in these effete modern times the historic cutting of the novice's finger for the signing in blood might prove unpopular, so he had mixed red ink with a little blue, thickened it slightly with cornstarch, put it in stoppered phials and called it Bull's Blood. The covenants, signed in this Bull's Blood, he retained. Duke's running expenses were exactly that—travel. He had no salaries to pay. The covens worked for pleasure. They provided their own black candles, black altar cloths, reversed crucifixes, or other trappings that took their fancy. They bought their own books, did their own research, brought their own food and drink to sabbath feasts, tried out their own spells, learned incantations and, should their imaginations become too free, a sharp reproof on Duke's next visit soon brought them into line. He had started his covens in Scotland as being the traditional hunting ground of witches and it was during a visit to the Glasgow coven that he had first met N.

Like Duke, N. too had read books and studied his chosen subject. He had explored the various idiocies in the name of this or that religion which had sprung up over the years, noting that the mainspring of each creed was the gospel that personal salvation could be bought for cash. As a prototype, he had picked on one which had been introduced by a man who had flourished by giving lectures for a short time in London's West End some thirty years before and whose books still sold well in America and occasionally in Britain. The blatant gibberish of these sermons had appealed to his cynical mind. To suit his purpose they needed little titivation, the main improvement necessary being a stronger emphasis on the ever-green and successful catchpenny that the way to true redemption lay through sin. There was nothing, N. had grasped, like a delicately tinted license to sin for bringing in the customers. His researchers had only heightened his conviction that people needed an assured man prepared to tell them what to do—and the more nonsensical the better—to give them clear-cut directions, rules and punishments, badges to make them feel they belonged to a brotherhood and the assurance that they themselves would be all right and never mind the rest. Provided that these ingredients were well mixed and well put over, there was almost no limit to what people would believe and, more important, no limit to what people then would pay. So Nuscience was born.

To anyone operating a witches' coven in Glasgow the Trossachs were an inevitable choice. All the traditional elements were present: water, trees and rocks. The last two features Duke could appreciate: trees aided concealment, and a good-size rock made a convenient focal point for the others to dance around and a commanding platform for himself. He himself had never seen the need for the proximity of water since it had no place in the ceremonies and, in spite of all his reading, he had never grasped that the ancient fertility rites applied principally to earth, not to human beings. However, the Trossachs were a suitable distance from the city: far enough to avoid interference by the authorities; near enough to be easily accessible by car.

In N.'s case the center of the city had to be his operating theater. He needed to hire a large hall and to arrange for publicity. From the beginning he had assumed for himself the title of Master and he had chosen the name Nuscience for his doctrine because, although he was aware of the automatic puns that would be made, an easy pun bred quick advertisement and in any case to become a nuisance was the sum of his intention. On this particular occasion he had determined to try out a new idea. All the more modern religions from Christianity onward had prophesied the end of the world at intervals; he saw no reason why his should lag behind and he had no objection to arranging an end to the world provided that it served his own ends. He had seen a way to achieve his object for a small outlay, his chief necessity being a large cave. He scoured the countryside and at length found what he wanted in the Trossachs. He had put it about among his adherents that the End of the World Was Nigh; just how Nigh he would divulge at his next lecture. Even he was surprised at the enthusiasm with which the rumor had been received. Human beings it would appear always welcomed the idea of total destruction and welcomed it even more ardently if they, as individuals, could be assured of an out. N. had stocked the cave with an impressive array of provisions, then had given his lecture, informing the congregation that by careful calculation he could now give them the exact date of Armageddon. The End of the World, he warned them, was due in a week's time. He proceeded to arrange with the best-heeled and most fervent of his disciples that they should retire to a Secret Place, bringing with them all their portable valuables, to await the event. As he had expected, the majority of them settled for money and jewels. They had been trained from childhood to worship money as their god, and he had foreseen that it was unlikely to occur to them that neither money nor jewels would avail them as a commercial asset after the holocaust.

N. received a jolt when a penitent member of his congregation confessed that she belonged to the local witches' coven and that on the following Friday night a sabbath was to take place in the Trossachs. After questioning her, he bought an animal mask, attended the sabbath and later succeeded in tracking the man who took the part of the Devil to a hotel in the city. N. called at the hotel next morning.

The two men had taken to each other at this first meeting. They had kindred natures, similar business methods and the same goal. There was no need for rivalry, indeed after a frank discussion they saw the advantages to be gained by combining their operations. Since neither man was a public company and each was the sole shareholder in his own concern there were no difficulties. A merger was arranged: Duke's organization would provide a perfect purging ground for any member of Nuscience who was in search of sin; while any straying sheep from the Devil's flock who had developed scruples could be sent to Nuscience to be revitalized and then returned to the Devil for a refresher course. As soon as their separate Glasgow enterprises were completed they would get down to details and plan schedules. Unfortunately there was a hitch.

When at the end of the prescribed time the devout nucleus from Nuscience emerged from their cave they found that the world had missed its date and was still spinning. Their total gain was two wasted weeks of discomfort; the loss of their valuables was also total. One hardheaded Glaswegian merchant, preferring to look a fool than be a sucker, complained to the police, who started an investigation. Fortunately for N., the merchant's wife was a member of the witches' coven. N. returned the lady's jewelry, though not the money, and Duke, who never attended a sabbath without a candid camera, called on her. He showed her some recent exposures of herself, thus securing her full cooperation. That evening her husband was found dead in his car, the garage doors closed, the engine still running. His wife attested that he had lately removed all her jewelry from the bank, which the police verified, and that her husband's complaint to the authorities had been the first step in an attempt to swindle his insurance company. She had been so shocked, she insisted, to learn of his intention that she had threatened to denounce him. The merchant's death was officially declared to be suicide and although the police were skeptical they were unable to take the matter further in view of the wife's sworn statement and the box of jewelry discovered hidden at the back of a wardrobe in the merchant's house.

The episode proved to Duke and N. the benefits of amalgamation; but the squeak had been narrow. It was evident that the end of the world needed more careful planning. Both N. and Duke decided that in future it would be wiser for them to work in the background and to engage a front man who could take the rap in case of trouble.

Since the Devil was always in disguise, one man could play both parts. They made inquiries and chose Hilary Evelyn, an actor who had drowned his career in the best of spirits. Duke and N. made good. They also made improvements. Lacking a manual for their creed, they concocted a work of fiction, tentatively entitled *The Beyond*, until N., knowing his public and feeling it did not go far enough, decided it should be *beyond* that. It became the textbook of Nuscience, to be plugged at every meeting. An important modification was that for the future all caves must have a second entrance. Their adherents' valuables should be put in a box to be sealed in front of witnesses and remain in full view throughout the time spent underground. It needed little knowledge of sleight of hand to remove the box and to substitute a dummy. It would remain optional to the faithful few as to whether, on their reemergence after the cataclysm, they should stay upon this earth and start repopulation, or whether they should take off for Elysian fields on other planets. When the box was officially opened and proved to be empty, it would be up to the few to increase their faith, to breathe even harder, and to follow their luggage, which had gone on in advance. N. and Duke picked a band of young men, called them Majordomes, trained them and paid them well to carry out all the preparatory work, to act as bodyguards and as keepers of the peace in both religions.

N. and Duke preferred to maintain a wide distance between each foray and, since their last campaign had been in Wales, Kent, where a witches' coven was already flourishing, had been elected as the placement of their next eruption.

Chapter 8

Nigel Colveden decided that he was making progress. For the first time in his nineteen years he had found a use for his removed cousin. At the end of the Maidstone meeting he had lost sight of the girl as the audience surged out, only to see her again near the main entrance talking to Basil Trenthorne. Nigel had breezed up to them, asked Basil tactlessly, How was crime? and forced an introduction. He had taken it from there. Of all the incredible luck to find that Merilee Paynel was actually staying in Plummergen at the George and Dragon. Nigel had insisted that it was his absolute duty as a resident to show her around and they were now ensconced at lunch in Brettenden's most expensive restaurant, where he seemed to be increasing his lead. Merilee ... Her parents must have been prophetic. She was the gayest and most amusing companion he'd ever met. He told her so.

She made a face. "Try living your life with a name like mine. Then on top of that to be dubbed the Merry Widow entails certain obligations, and while it's excusable to fail your friends, it's unpardonable to disappoint your enemies."

Nigel was disconcerted. "Basil only said Merilee Paynel; I'm sorry but I didn't know it was Mrs.—that you'd been married."

"How should you? You don't know anything about me. And the stigma of marriage doesn't necessarily leave visible stigmata." Nigel tried to question, to find out more. She evaded. Nothing, she declared, was so boring as the recital of another's dullness. The waitress cleared their plates. He ordered coffee. Mrs. Paynel leaned back and took out her cigarette case. Quickly Nigel lit a match and bent forward.

"You—dull?"

She inhaled, blew a smoke ring and smiled. "You'll learn the only intriguing people are the ones you never know."

"You talk like a book."

"What harm? I've eyes to read." She reversed the conversation and questioned him.

"My life?" He grinned. "Just ... dull."

"Oh, come," she mocked, "it's early yet; you've still got time. I don't think the pattern forms before you're twenty; you're still in the melting pot. You could explore—I don't know what, but there must be things still longing to be found. You could carry a briefcase and wear a bowler hat."

"Or stay a farmer, which is what I like."

"You could do that, become a scientist, or get religion."

"Do you really belong to Nuscience?" he asked.

"I belong ... to myself." She stubbed her cigarette and took another, which he lit. " 'With no motor but the mind,' " she mimicked. "I'm all for cheaper travel, but somehow I don't think my mind's properly geared."

"But you were at the meeting," Nigel objected.

"So were you; but I didn't take it for granted you belonged."

"What"—he was puzzled—"brought someone like you to an off-the-track little place like Plummergen?"

"My car."

He persisted. "Yes, but I mean—"

"Meaning?" She cut him short. "Why must meanings have a meaning?" She refilled their cups. "Tell me, what's it like to live in a tiny village?"

Nigel shrugged. "Just like that. Everybody knows everything you do, and if you change your brand of toothpaste it's a sensation."

"Who's your local artist?" she inquired.

"Local …?" He shook his head. "Haven't got one."

"Yes you have. I saw her down by the coast, painting."

"Oh." He chuckled. "That would be our Miss Seeton; she's a drawing teacher. She's taking the schoolkids on an outing by the sea today."

"But this wasn't today. And she was alone."

"That would be her. There's been a splendid row about it. Some of the parents don't think she's fit to be in charge of their little horrors because half the village has suddenly upped and decided she's a witch."

"Have they?" He put down his cup; looked up surprised at her change of tone. "And is she?" she asked.

He grinned. "I wouldn't put anything past her, the way she hops in and out of scrapes. I expect she was having a first look over the ground and doing a picture of the sea as a sample for the kids."

"But she didn't," Merilee Paynel said slowly. "She drew the church."

"What church?"

Impatiently: "The church by the wood, of course."

"She couldn't have," protested Nigel. "That's near Iverhurst, further inland—must be a good mile away."

She put her cigarette case back in her bag and stood up abruptly. "Churches bore me, they're so righteous and rectangular."

He signaled for the bill. "Are you free tomorrow night?"

"No. I've an engagement."

Nigel, with visions of Basil, spoke without thinking. "Who with? Couldn't you break it?"

In a flash of irritation: "To sup with the Devil with a long spoon—and I never break engagements." Then she softened. "Perhaps some other night."

"Do you dance?" he questioned eagerly.

"Reasonably. Given sufficient reason."

There was a hunt ball the following Saturday, just outside of Maidstone. Would she go with him? She would. Nigel paid the bill in a happy haze and drove her back in the little red M.G. that he had inherited from his mother.

The girl broke a long silence. "Why a witch?"

"A witch?" He had to collect his thoughts. "Oh, you mean Miss Seeton. God knows; I don't. All I do know is, if she's a witch and I was the Devil I'd stay downstairs—it'd be safer."

How very worrying. Miss Seeton searched. The portfolio was the only likely place and, indeed, she was almost certain she remembered putting it there. But evidently not. All her other sketches were here, including one, in fact, which, now she came to look at it, was completely unfamiliar. She studied it. Very slapdash, she was afraid. Just a brief note of a rather desolate-looking church with trees behind it. Well, of course, they weren't properly drawn, only smudged in—it looked really more like a large wood. Yes, that would be it. A quick impression of something that she'd seen, somewhere, at some time, and had put down so as not to forget it. Meaning to work on it later. And now she had. Forgotten it, that was.

Miss Seeton retied the tapes of the cardboard folder and pushed it back into the bottom drawer of her writing desk. She got up from her knees.

Well, it couldn't be helped. She'd have to do without it. She'd manage time to make another sketch of the view this afternoon, while overseeing the children. If it was to be a competition, there must, she felt, be one accurate representation; something one could use as a standard for comparison. Now, did she have everything she needed? Her sketching frame, pencils, brushes, paints, scissors, some colored magazines and paste. And—oh, yes, she'd had a feeling she'd remembered she'd forgotten something—that notebook she'd always kept with pieces of material pressed flat between the leaves. Yes, that was all. Oh, no. It wasn't. She'd quite forgotten lunch. Miss Seeton hurried to the kitchen and collected the Thermos flask and sandwiches that Martha had prepared for her. Yes, that truly was all. She could safely say that now she was ready.

"Miss." "Please, miss." "If you please, miss."

Miss Seeton went from one to another, discussing, proffering advice, discussing again and sometimes, when asked to, making a correction. One ten-year-old sat staring at the view, her paper blank. Miss Seeton squatted cross-legged on the grass beside her and looked out to sea. Finally the child spoke.

"Can't draw it and don' wan' to."

"No?" Miss Seeton smiled. "Doesn't it mean anything?"

"Oh, yes," the girl replied with fervor. "It means"—she struggled—"means words to me, not drawing; don' like drawing."

"You don't have to. Painting is only a method of putting down impressions; of trying to tell others what you've seen. There are lots of ways of doing it. Building and modeling, and writing; even just remembering, but that perhaps is rather selfish because it entails keeping it entirely to yourself. And then sometimes one forgets."

"You mean"—the girl turned to her eagerly—"you mean I could write it?"

"Why not?" Miss Seeton rose. "It's just as good a means as any other."

One small boy was sitting, mutinous. His paper too was blank. Miss Seeton stood behind him. He fidgeted.

"Drawin' an' paintin's sissy," he told her. "Me"—two small hands screwed together—"I like t' make things."

"Well, do that," said Miss Seeton. She brought him the glossy magazines, the notebook with material scraps, the scissors and the paste.

"But y' can't do all that." He waved a hand at the view. " 'S too big."

"Then make a frame of your fingers and look through it. Choose the bit you like, and if you want a smaller picture hold your hands farther away."

He tried it grudgingly; became interested. "If you do that," he explained to her, "y' get a proper picture in a frame."

"Good," said Miss Seeton. "Then you choose a color for a bit you want, cut it the right shape, stick it down, and then work on from there."

He looked at the magazines. "How'd I know to cut it right?"

"Well, one way," she suggested, "is to draw an outline." She sketched one lightly on his paper. "Say that's that strip of grass; then you cut a piece to fit. Or"—she produced some—"you can use tracing paper."

Within a few minutes he was hard at work. Some of the others grew jealous and intrigued. Could they stick things on theirs? Miss Seeton encouraged them: Why not? She crossed the grass to look over the shoulder of the budding authoress.

The sea, the sky,	The grass and stones
The sea, the sky	Are here and nere
Are far away,	And wen they stop
They never stop.	They drop.

They drop to sand were shells begin,
Then sea with fish that swim away
To meet the sky with birds that fly
But never stop.

"That," observed Miss Seeton, "is one of the best pictures I've seen."

Everyone appeared to be occupied for the moment and her own sketch was finished and put away. Miss Seeton took her handbag and umbrella and looked around. Would they, she wondered, finish before the bus arrived to take them home, and need another view? Over there was a possible vantage point, where there was that rise in the ground. On reaching the mound she discovered that the rise was more abrupt than she had thought. To help herself gain a foothold she used her umbrella as a lever. The umbrella point sank into the ground.

Surely it was very soft. Crumbly, in fact. One didn't want the children with sprained ankles. By the way of experiment she prodded the earth hard. Yes, she was quite right. It was crumbly. She could feel the vibration and the shift beneath her feet. Well, first she'd see if the view from the mound was worth it. And, if it was, one could probably find another route. She raised one foot and leaned her weight on her umbrella; but instead of Miss Seeton going up, the umbrella went down as the abused earth disintegrated beneath her and fell away with a patter of soil and stones to leave a gaping hole. There was time for gasped surprise and one small cry of shocked dismay before Miss Seeton disappeared.

Chapter 9

Miss Seeton opened her eyes. And closed them quickly: so very bright. She waited until the discomfort of her position became palpable, then opened her eyes again and saw the sky. The sky? she blinked several times. The sky remained. She managed to sit up and look about her: memory returned. Really. How very careless. She should have foreseen … She flexed and felt. No, nothing seemed amiss. Except for one's head, of course. Gingerly she explored the back of her head. And even that might have been worse. A slight swelling, a little painful; but her hat had saved her. Which was more than she deserved. So very stupid. Worrying about the children spraining things and to forget that one was equally vulnerable. She picked herself up and dusted at her clothes. It made her sneeze. Well—having fallen in, she must now climb out. She searched and recovered her handbag and umbrella, then looked above her. Rather far above. As best she could, she pushed some of the loose rubble into a pile and climbed upon it. Yes, now she could get the handle of her umbrella over the edge. If she could hook it there and pull …? She pulled. She got more rubble and a bigger hole. When she had finished coughing and the air had cleared she looked at her watch. It didn't appear to be broken. A quarter to four? She put it to her ear. Yes, it was still going. Good heavens, the bus was due in half an hour. And the children might be wondering. She must get out at once. She took stock of her position. She wasn't exactly in a hole. At least only in one sense. For the hole continued in one direction as a passage. But it was too dark to see how far it went. Well, one might, of course, have to try it as a last resort. But first she must make sure. It ought to be possible to get out the way she had come in. A wall of rubble faced her. She stepped upon it. It gave way, disturbing dust. She stood back and considered. Was there a better place? Yes. Here, where that large stone was, looked more promising. It held her weight. She scrambled up a little way, her foot slipped and she slid to base, landing with a bump.

"Oh, bother," said Miss Seeton.

Two young men were at work in an underground chamber. Their work was deceptive. On a shelf which ran the length of one side of the huge cellar they were stacking tinned provisions—the cheaper varieties. As each carton of tins was emptied, they resealed it and placed it on the shelf, behind its erstwhile contents. It was in this that their labor was calculated to deceive; giving a double impression for a single expenditure.

One of them dragged forward a heavy crate of bottles. He lined the bottles up on the rock floor and tossed the empty crate up to his companion. Stooping had made his face throb and he stroked a swelling across the bridge of his nose with heedful fingers. He wore a black plastic ring.

"James."

"Huh?"

"What really was that do at the meeting all in aid of?"

"The old girl was with that detective we chucked out," James explained, "and she'd been taking notes. Duke wanted to check."

"Well, next time he wants to check on somebody's grandmother he can do it himself. Old biddies with brollies weren't on my combat course. No rough stuff, Duke says. Why the hell didn't somebody tell her that? Looked as mild as milk, but I'd no sooner got a grip on her bag when, wham! she bashes me in the face and starts laying about her in all directions."

James was bored with complaints. "Stow it, Ted, and fetch the empties."

Ted crossed to a corner of the cellar, gathered armfuls of empty bottles and brought them over. "Need to fill these?"

"No." James began to drop them in the crate. "With their tops on they look all right. Who's going to reach over and pinch one out of this lot when the full ones are easier to get at? And we'd need to go all the way up top for water."

"Why couldn't they have laid it on down here?" Ted grumbled. "Thought smuggling was supposed to be so well organized."

"There wasn't laid-on water in those days. What would smugglers want with water anyway? They came up the tunnel, stored their cargo here and then, if the Excise were about and they had to hole up, they could always breach a keg or so of brandy. Besides, we don't want too much weight on the shelves—we'll have the damn things down."

In a corner, near the roof, a bell rang. They stopped and watched. The bell was one of three, hung one above the other.

The top bell rang twice more. They relaxed. A door at one end of the cellar opened and Basil Trenthorne carried in a suitcase.

"Sorry I'm late." He received sour looks. "Had to get some stuff for a new idea Duke's dreamed up for tomorrow night."

"Where'd you leave the car?" asked James.

"Didn't. Duke dropped me. He's not taking any risks round here at the moment. Had to walk down through the blasted wood—brambles everywhere. You can't even see the church from that path you cut till you've taken a purler over a couple of gravestones. He'll have us picked up soon as it's dark." He smirked at Ted. "There's a job lined up for you."

"Me? Why me? It's always me." Ted slammed the last of the bottles into the crate. "Got enough to do tarting this place up to look like a grocer's shop. Any new jobs, you do 'em. Wouldn't hurt you to dirty your lily whites for once."

"Not my line," Basil sneered. "Spot of burglary with trimmings. Duke says you can look the place over this evening and do the job tomorrow night."

"Do what? Where?"

Basil smiled maliciously. "Plummergen. You should be grateful," he jibed. "Duke's offering you a return match with the old geezer who biffed you on the snout and made it all uneven. Not that you're in her class ..." He skipped back as Ted swung at him.

James caught Ted's arm. "Stuff it, both of you. What's the old girl done that Duke's so worked up about? After all, she only turned out to be the aunt of that gorilla who drove her home."

"Aunt, nothing. That was an act. And the gorilla happens to be a Yard man."

James freed Ted. "The Yard?"

Basil was pleased with himself. "I asked around a bit. She's worked with the Yard; she's well known; she's the one the papers call the Battling Brolly."

"Where'd you get all this?"

"Mother's been staying with some duff cousins of ours in the village; they all know about this Miss Seeton there."

"But if she's in with the police," James objected, "they'll have the notebook already; so where's the point?"

Basil condescended. "The point, my dear James, is that the notebook's not the half of it. It looks as if she's on to this place." He observed their reactions with relish. "The day Merilee arrived, she met the old trout down by the coast. The Brolly was pretending to paint the view, but Merilee saw the picture and it was this church—plus the wood behind it—and it's not even in sight from where she was. So what's the betting she was hunting for the tunnel? Duke's hopping. Says you're to find the picture and get it. Get her at the same time." He laughed. "Nothing violent, of course. Just enough to put her in hospital for a bit—and if she turns up dead on arrival he won't lose any sleep. Can't afford to have her rummaging about for the next few weeks until we've finished here."

Ted's expression was mulish. "And what's this new gammon for tomorrow night?" he demanded. "More work?"

"Not much," Basil reassured him. "You know that platform thing they must've used to raise the barrels on, under the trapdoor; he wants us to get it working. I've brought some rope. We've got to shove the Master through it at the crucial moment. I've got his gear in this." He tapped the suitcase and laughed. "I've also got a little idea of my own which should wake his devilship up."

"What?" James wanted to know.

Basil looked sly. "Never mind. Just a small touch of reality which should get old Hilary in the proper mood and keep him on his toes. Duke wants us to have some colored lights shining underneath the trap."

Ted's surliness increased. "Why?"

"Because he thinks it'll help to give 'em all the heebies. When we wind his highness up as the service starts, it'll look like Old Nick coming up from his home town."

"Why?" repeated Ted. "Doing all right as we are, aren't we?"

"Duke wants the pace hotted up a bit now that we're near the end of this one."

Ted was unappeased. "Pity they got themselves chased out of Malebury. Now we've got the two things together, one on top of the other. I don't care how phony it is, black magic's not a thing to muck about with. One day they'll really raise the Devil by mistake, and then where'll we all be?"

"Oh, belt up," said James. "Let's get on."

They carried a butane gas lantern up two shallow steps to a smaller cellar and set to work. They fixed new rope to the reel of a winch that controlled a loading platform, threaded it through the pulleys, oiled all the mechanism. James stood on a box and worked the rusted iron bolt which secured the ceiling trap until it moved silently, then pulled it free, letting a heavy stone slab swing slowly on its iron pivot, balanced by a counterweight. The edge of the stone flicked against a wire running across the roof: a bell rang. The other two jumped nervously and Ted headed for the main cellar.

"All right—hold it," James calmed them. "Only me. We'll have to shift the wire farther over. Nobody warned me we might need this damned trap."

Between them he and Ted moved the wire, Basil handing up tools. It took time since the staples had to be rawlplugged into rock and the wire reset with springs at intervals of its length to keep the tension. They had fitted this alarm system to all three entrances of the smugglers' old hideout. The top bell was connected to the entrance from the crypt of the ancient church outside Iverhurst. The second was wired the full length of over a mile down the slope of the main tunnel, which ended in a cave at the cliff face, the mouth concealed by rocks and still occasionally awash during a spring tide. The third entrance, hidden by boulders and scrub, was on the downs; this was a branch tunnel which joined the main one a quarter of a mile below the church. Their rewiring completed, Basil was sent to test it. Taking his flashlight, he went up a short passage which ended in a rough wall, put his hand on one of the irregular pieces of stone and pushed it sideways to release a catch. He leaned his weight against the wall. A section swiveled, pivoting on the same principle as the trap. The bell rang. He flicked the wire twice to complete their usual signal, pushed the section back into place and rejoined the others. James gripped the edges of the roof opening, swung himself up and through and stood for a few moments behind the altar rail. Yes—it could work. Effective too, with the church lit only by a few black candles, and the Devil rising slowly by the altar in a ghostly light—providing the old devil wasn't drunk again and didn't fall back into the pit.

"Right," he called down. "Try her out."

Ted worked the winch handle. The platform rose smoothly until at full extent it fitted the opening a bare half inch below the sanctuary floor. James stepped onto it and was lowered. They stopped the contraption before the bottom to test the ratchet brake and to give James time to close the trap and shoot the bolt. Leaving Basil's suitcase there, they returned to the main cellar and continued to unpack the foodstuffs.

A bell rang. They froze. They watched it as it swung still at the end of its wire. James jumped forward and put out the lamp. All three flicked on their flashlights.

Basil was shaken. "What the devil …?"

"Be quiet," rapped James.

He kept his flashlight trained on the wire near the bell. Little more than a minute later the wire jerked and the bell rang again. They waited. There was no third ring. They hurried the length of the cellar and stepped down into the last of the three chambers, quite small, almost an antechamber. They grouped themselves near the wall on the far side and listened. They heard nothing.

"Put out your lights. And, Ted, you slip through." "Why me?"

"Don't argue. Go down and see if you can find out what's happening. We'll leave the slab open a crack so you can get back quickly if you have to." James pressed on a protruding piece of rock, thrust against the wall, a part of which swung outward, a replica of the one in the crypt. "And don't," he added, "use a light more than you need."

After his third fall in the dark on the uneven floor, Ted decided to use his own discretion; he switched on his flashlight and sped on his unwilling way. Time enough to turn off the glim when he saw reason for it. Past the branch to the Downs—no sign of trouble there. The way was easier now, more sand, but he was getting blown. He eased his pace—he was no three-minute-miler. Finally ahead of him he saw a faint light. He switched off the flashlight and approached with caution. Dust, carried on a current of air, half choked him, making his eyes water. Finally his progress was blocked by a pile of debris above which, through a crack, he could just see the sky. So that was it—the roof had fallen in. More work. They'd probably be kept up half the night reshoring it. Beyond the blockage he heard a sound. He flattened against the tunnel wall and listened. Dust tickled his nose; he longed to sneeze. The sound came again; a scrabbling noise. He let his breath go in a sigh of relief. A sheep—like the one that had tripped the wire at the opening on the Downs the other day. Some old sheep must have trodden on a weak patch and fallen through. They'd have to get it out. If it was missed and somebody started looking, the tunnel might be spotted before it could be repaired. Why let the stupid animals wander around loose? Always causing trouble. Probably broken its fool leg—hadn't moved again. He listened for some sign of life from the sheep on the other side. Had it upped and died? As if in answer the scrabbling came again, then a sliding rattle, followed by a bump.

"Oh, bother," said the old sheep on the other side.

Well, that was that, Miss Seeton decided. She'd have to try the passage. So while the startled Ted raced one way, to warn the others and get help, Miss Seeton went the other.

Away from the hole, darkness closed in on her. Miss Seeton stopped. She needed … Oh, how very fortunate. One country custom that she had acquired was always to carry a small flashlight in her bag. She found it and switched it on. It showed a narrow passage with a downward slant. The child's poem came to her mind.

> The grass and stones
> Something something
> And when they stop
> They drop.
> They drop to sand …

Of course. That would be it. This would be some passage—part of a cave, or, perhaps, joining one, which should, if she was lucky, lead straight down to the sea. Well, not, one trusted, literally to the sea, but to the beach. The coast round this part of the country was honeycombed with such caves and tunnels, she believed. All along here as far as Dover and beyond. And, of course, Romney Marsh had been notorious for smugglers in olden days. She moved forward with confidence. This passage would, she now felt sure, unquestionably "drop to sand." Her confidence was justified: the tunnel widened, became a small cave with daylight showing through an opening at the farther end. Miss Seeton crossed the uneven rocky floor, put her flashlight back into her handbag and clambered past rocks and boulders overhung by stunted bushes onto sand. Now. How to get back? She took a few steps, then turned to face the dunes. It shouldn't be too difficult. If she climbed up, as straight as she could manage, she should, surely, come out near where the children were. She looked back to mark the entrance to the cave. It had vanished. Sand, rocks and boulders, stunted shrubs and coarse grass faced her in a broken line for as far as she could see. Well, never mind, it didn't matter, she'd no intention of returning. Miss Seeton set off up the dunes.

"If you please, miss." "Please, miss." "Miss, can I ...?" "*Miss* ..."

The children began to wonder. They didn't ought, was the consensus of opinion, to be left on their own like this—they might get up to something. The child poetess remembered that she'd seen Miss go thataway. They all downed tools and went in search of her. They came to the mound.

"Now mind where you're going, Emmie, mind your feet, 's dangerous."

" 'S gone an' given way, 's fallen in."

"Look, there's a great big hole."

They gathered round in a respectful group.

"She down there?"

"Must be."

"Think she's copped it?"

"Must've, else she'd holler."

A little girl began to cry.

"Now stow it, Liz, 'spec' she's just knocked silly."

The boy who had learned to cut out pictures crawled to the edge; looked down. Friends held his legs.

"Not there," he reported, " 'less she's under all that muck." Liz wailed anew.

"Best get the driver," one of them suggested.

"Children, the bus is here."

They turned, dumbfounded. Miss Seeton stood behind them: handbag on her arm, umbrella in her hand, her hat squashed and crooked, her clothes slightly torn, sand spilling from her shoes and all of her dusty and disheveled. She stood there smiling. They stared back in awe.

"Now come along. We mustn't keep the driver waiting."

She led the way: the children followed. None of them liked to question her. It was obvious what had taken place. This was the right sort of teacher—no mistake. One who could pop down into the ground whenever she'd a mind, do whatever it was that she got up to there, go flying out to sea, fly all around and back again, come bobbing up behind you just when you knew as she weren't there. Too right they'd been—didn't half need to watch your step with this one. They trooped after her in silence, imbued with a new respect. For one whole Plummergen generation Miss Seeton's reputation was decreed.

Chapter 10

Mrs. Blaine was taking her duties seriously, and following the Maidstone meeting, she had felt quite inspired. She and Miss Nuttel after much discussion had decided to put salvation before cash consideration and had joined Nuscience. They had even, though "this was too secret," been allowed to hear hints of the Secret Place. Now with two friends, in search of guidance, they were gathered for a table-rapping séance after supper. Hands spread on a small polished table, their thumbs and little fingers touching, the room lit only by a shaded lamp, they sat and waited. And waited. Eventually Mrs. Blaine, always short-suffering, demanded to know if anyone was there. The table, taken by surprise, gave a start and rocked. Thrilled, they confirmed the code: three raps for Yes and one for No and the letters of the alphabet by numbers.

Once it had got the hang of things the table joined the spirit of the game. It tapped out messages, although it couldn't spell and was inclined to stop mid-sentence as though forgetful of its theme. The quickest and surest method appeared to be question and answer. Was Miss Seeton a witch? The table said she was. Was there danger all about them? The table was sure of it. Was the church at Iverhurst bedeviled with ghosts? Yes: the table was emphatic. Wasn't it their duty to insist that something should be done? The table nearly broke a leg insisting that it should.

The party finished late, good nights were exchanged and the ladies retired to rest enkindled afresh with missionary zeal. They were to be the saviors of the district and Mrs. Blaine felt all too keenly her position as the leader of the band.

She visited the Brettenden Free Library; read a book. If the district was to be infested with eerie lights which appeared in empty churches at midnight, with ghosts and witches, the district, as the Master had too rightly said, must then he purged, and this book, *Ghosts and Go-Betweens*, told you just too clearly how to do it. You had to exorcise them. An ordained priest, it stipulated, was necessary to perform this feat.

Mrs. Blaine and Miss Nuttel canvassed the village; exhorting, arguing, demanding. Finally, when sufficient enthusiasm had been roused, they led a deputation to the vicarage. There they met with opposition.

Miss Treeves was adamant. Never, she averred, had she heard such foolishness. Nor would she dream of letting Arthur get entangled. And table rapping … Really, she had no patience. How could they be so silly? And as for the suggestion that Arthur should go to Iverhurst, at night, and exorcise … It was quite the stupidest idea she'd ever heard. And if there really were lights at Iverhurst, then it was a matter for the police.

"You don't understand," protested Norah Blaine. "Even if the police would take it seriously—which of course they never do—there's nothing they can do against evil spirits. It's too obviously a matter for the Church; it says so here." She produced the library book. Wisely, knowing Miss Treeves' sympathies, she had avoided the subject of Miss Seeton.

The vicar listened and felt unhappy. Molly was right, of course. She always was. And it did all sound unlikely and farfetched. Spirits … Well, frankly he knew nothing of them. And as for exorcising … He'd heard of it, of course. Yes, yes, of course he had; he'd read of it in books. And in the Bible the casting out of devils was referred to many times. But to the best of his recollection it didn't mention the procedure. Presumably there must be some kind of ceremony. He really didn't see … But on the other hand, these were his parishioners, and he was responsible for their welfare. And Iverhurst church, though never used, did lie within his parish. But even so, he didn't see … It was very difficult.

Sensing his weakness, Mrs. Blaine attacked. "It's too clear that it's your duty, vicar. You're the only one can save us. It's always the Church that has to do it—haunted houses or anything like that. Spirits and ghosts don't pay attention to ordinary people, but when the Church commands they must obey. It's all in here." She waved the book. "It says 'Evil spirits flee when exorcised' on page ninety-four. You can't possibly leave things as they are—it would be too dreadful."

"Won't do," agreed Miss Nuttel.

Arthur Treeves looked hunted. "I … er …" he began.

"Arthur …" warned his sister.

"It's—that I don't know about such things," he confessed. "I don't know how to exorcise. I—I believe there's a special ministry that deals with exorcism. I'd have to inquire."

"No need for outsiders," said Miss Nuttel. "Waste of time."

"It's all in here." Mrs. Blaine handed him *Ghosts and Go-Betweens*. "In chapter twelve; it's too simple. You hold a sort of service and sprinkle holy water to consecrate the ground, and make the sign of the cross and things like that. And then you command the spirits to go away and say—"

"Avaunt," supplied Miss Nuttel.

The deputation won. Miss Treeves fought a rearguard action. If this folly was to be done at all, it must be done by day. They wouldn't hear of it. It said in *Ghosts and Go-Betweens* that the most successful time for exorcising was at the same hour that spirits had appeared. The book apparently made a point of this; possibly on the assumption that if the spirits were not there to hear they might not get the message.

The project was determined and the deputation left. Once they had got their way their enthusiasm mounted. A nucleus of them decided that the vicar must have support: they would accompany him to see the job was done. The idea caught on and flashed around the village. Nearly everyone would go—it wasn't the sort of things to miss. Should be better than the Harvest Festival. It was discussed among those who owned cars who should lift whom; some would go on bicycles; some would make up parties, starting early, and proceed on foot. Flasks were filled with tea, and sandwiches were cut. It was arranged with their mothers that the church choir should have their tea early and be sent to bed; to be roused later with cups of cocoa and with sugared buns—the baker did a sellout—so that they could be there on time to lead the community, at the right moment, in the singing of a hymn. The village looked forward to the best treat in months. Even Sir George, informed by Molly Treeves of what was brewing, decided the padre might need bolstering. And anyway, as Nigel said, if they were set on this damnfool thing, why miss the fun?

Could he get a transfer, Foxon wondered? Much more of this and he'd had it in the force. Poor little thing. First that meeting, and now to drag an elderly party out on a September night to sit in an abandoned church and catch a cold, in case she got impressions. She'd get pneumonia, that was what. He didn't care if she was being paid for it, they'd no right to do it. And no complaints: just seemed to think she ought to do whatever she was told. Well, it was wrong. Old Brimmers ought to have his head examined. She was—what was the word?—gallant; that was it. Foxon boiled. Well, he'd done his best. He'd looked over her getup for the jaunt and said it wouldn't do. He'd borrowed an old blue duffel coat from the local P.C.'s, Potter's, wife and insisted that she wear it. It was much too big for her. And if she put the hood up she'd be snuffed out like a candle. But at least she might keep warm. He'd pinched a leather cushion too to try and make her comfortable. But there really wasn't much you could do except to get it over with. He backed down the path to the church door, holding a flashlight to guide her footsteps. Trailing blue melton cloth, Miss Seeton followed him.

A bend in the path took Foxon by surprise. He trod on grass, on a gravestone, did an ungainly dance and crashed. So did the flashlight, which smashed. Heroically he muffled both his feelings and his words. "Don't fall over your feet" had been his first injunction. Well, he'd done that. Next on the list was to knock the building down.

Miss Seeton was distressed. "Oh, poor Mr. Foxon, did you hurt herself?"

"No, not a bit," he lied. "I only broke a couple of my backs. Pity about the flashlight—we'll have to crawl the rest."

Miss Seeton fumbled beneath the navy blue, found her bag and opened it. Really, one did appreciate why country people ... She produced her flashlight. A thin pencil of light pierced the surrounding darkness and, thus enlightened, they proceeded on their way.

Once they were inside the church, Miss Seeton's flashlight proved less than adequate. It found the way to the main aisle, described the jutting carving on a pew, but failed to warn their feet of moldering hassocks. Miss·Seeton and Foxon groped and stumbled on until they reached the center of the building. Foxon tried a pew for comfort. It lacked it. The hard, narrow seat, the upright back, would prove impossible after a short time. The only impression anyone would get would be one of numbness in the nub. He left Miss Seeton there while he explored. The pulpit was useless since the stairs were rotten. Returning to the nave, he passed the choir stalls until the thin flashlight beam showed the gap in the center of the communion rail. Ahead must lie the high altar, which wouldn't help, and so he tried the sides. To his right he found the mildewed remains of tapestry lying on the floor. He shone the light above and saw a brass rod, from which the tapestry had fallen, protruding at a drunken angle from a pillar which was set against the wall. The left-hand side was better. The tapestry here still clung precariously to its rod. Evidently they had once framed the extremities of the sanctuary steps, hiding such mundane things as a door, a row of pegs and two stools, one with a missing leg. He fetched Miss Seeton and asked her where she'd rather sit: against the wall? or out in the open?

Miss Seeton was uncertain; uncertain where to sit; uncertain quite what was required of her. Foxon explained once more that the chief inspector was anxious that she should remain for a while and feel the atmosphere of the church at night—get an impression. Miss Seeton was dubious. It was, she pointed out, a little difficult, perhaps, in some ways, to gain an exact impression of a church that one could not see. But supposing that one were lucky, on the other hand, and the moon came out, one might then, of course, be able to see the buildings as a whole. So it would be wiser, in that case, to sit forward a little, where one would have the chance to do so, supposing that one were. Lucky, she meant.

Foxon pulled out the sound stool, dusted it with his sleeve and set it behind the edge of the tapestry, hoping that the tattered relic might help to keep some drafts at bay. He arranged the cushion and settled Miss Seeton. He searched and found the missing leg to the other stool, propped it in the angle formed by the wall and pillar, sat down and resigned himself to patience.

Death and the Queen of Hearts—and soon. Miss Wicks pulled the woollen wrap tighter round her shoulders. Whom could it signify? It was silly to be scared, since foreseeing by cards was essentially only a sort of solitaire, but this was the sixth sequence in succession and the message was the same— the Ace of Spades next to the Queen of Hearts. And soon. It seemed so sinister. Should she stop?

The old lady gathered up the cards and reshuffled the pack. She was, as she often was, alone. People tended to avoid private conversation with Miss Wicks. Like many individuals with a speech defect, she appeared to be under a compulsion to practice the impracticable and the effect of her protruding teeth and the constant stream of *s*'s which sissed through them was mesmeric. Notwithstanding their efforts, others would find their own upper lips beginning to twitch, retract, and they in their turn would start to hiss unlooked-for *s*'s in response. Even in silence a subtle essence of sibilance seemed to surround Miss Wicks.

Tentative, worried, the old lady again began to lay out the cards. The Queen of Clubs. She felt happier. At least since that was not the same the rest also should be dissimilar. Encouraged, she laid down another card and referred to her copy of *Master Metaphysics* to find the meaning. The Place Card ... Here it was—House. The Queen of Clubs in her house. The following card according to the book typified the Law. The Queen of Clubs in her house and associated with the law? That must surely stand for Miss Seeton: no one else of her acquaintance had any association with the law—the police. This was most exciting. Quickly she took the top card, peeped at it; wavered. The Ace of Spades. Reluctantly she put it down and brooded on the resultant formation. Yes, there was a difference: the Ace was in reverse. Surely that symbolized something else. She consulted the book again: the Ace of Spades reversed was Accident. Unless ... Was it possible she had reversed it by mistake? In which case it was Death. With misgiving she turned the final card, the Time Card. This meant ... no, she must ask the book. The book replied: Immediate; At Once.

Old Miss Wicks pushed the table from her and levered herself to her feet. It was most disturbing, because there was no one about; the whole village was at Iverhurst for the exorcism. And if Miss Seeton were seriously menaced in her own house, and anything should take place, she would feel so responsible. Miss Seeton, so sane and sensible, was the least likely person to have set off for the exorcism, and there was no question strange things did take place in Miss Seeton's vicinity. The clock on the mantel gave one chime. A quarter past eleven. It was very late for visiting, but without a telephone there was no other means of making certain and at least if nothing was amiss Miss Seeton was not the sort to scoff or make her feel ridiculous.

By this time the old lady had buttoned herself into her mouton mink coat. She pulled on her daisy hat, a home-knitted affair, which resembled a tea cozy with a pompon on top made from a superabundance of yellow and white wool scraps. It looked like a prize-winning chrysanthemum, but to Miss Wicks it was a daisy and she was proud of it. Allowing for shrinkage she had made the hat too big, so for safety she placed a scarf over it and tied it beneath her chin. She drew on her gloves, picked up her handbag, locked the front door behind her and, flashlight in one hand, her cane in the other, four inches of matchstick leg exposed beneath mouton mink, long pointed shoes neatly splayed in divergent directions, Miss Wicks embarked upon her thirty-yard expedition down the street.

On her arrival at Sweetbriars she found the cottage in darkness, the front door ajar. This daunted her. She stepped back and looked around for help. All the other houses showed dark and silent, reminding her that everyone had gone to Iverhurst. Fearful, she pushed the door wide and shone her flashlight into the passage. It was empty; no sound, no sign of anyone. She faltered forward, stepped through the doorway on her right into Miss Seeton's sitting room, played the beam of light upon the wall, found the switch and stretched out her hand as a beam of light brighter than hers sprang from behind her. She gasped and was about to turn, when she felt rather than heard a swishing in the air and a blow upon her head put out all lights for her.

Chapter 11

Ted, anonymous in motorcycle gear, wheeled his machine off the road across the Downs and parked it behind some scrub. By the beam of his powerful flashlight he picked his way past an assortment of cars. Looked like most of them'd arrived. His mouth set in a mutinous line. What did N. and Duke want to mess about with witchcraft for? Doing well enough on Nuscience, weren't they? And this new prank of bringing the witch lot up through the caves—crackers. If they didn't want cars parked near the church, why use it? Go a mile or two farther on and use the wood. But no, Duke liked to use a church if there was one handy; said it gave a service that extra something. It'd give it good night if he wasn't careful. And the hell of a secret the Nuscientists' Secret Place was going to be with half of Kent traipsing back and forth through it. And, Ted reflected bitterly, the extra work. Tacking up black sheeting everywhere so that all the witches and warlocks didn't get an eyeful of what they weren't supposed to. Nuscience itself was good straight stuff: cod the fools, take their money, soak the richest of 'em with this Secret Place stuff and then get out. But devil worship, no. Start fooling about with odd Powers and you'd find one day the Powers were a bit odder than you thought. Involuntarily his shoulders contracted. He had a feeling there was trouble coming. Look at that old soak Evelyn, already more than half believing the crap he spouted. If they kept him playing the Devil much longer he'd grow himself a pair of horns for real—and a tail. Ted pushed his way through some bushes to where the boulder had been rolled back from the passage entrance.

In the smaller cellar, underneath the sanctuary, Ted pulled aside the black material to find that the lamp was lit and that James and another Majordome were kneeling on the floor throwing dice, while Hilary Evelyn, black-robed, a piece of paper in one hand, strode to and fro declaiming, "*Deum nostrum hoc ad* ..." A part of the actor's mind was on his lines as he repeated Latin in reverse and the rest was concentrated on his power. Deriding Power from Above, you gained Power from Below. Which power was greatest? Could base power defy the power Sublime and win? His fingers plucked nervously at his robe, but in removing his jacket he had removed his flask. The answer for him, as all answers spiritual, was spirituous.

Ted crossed to the others. James glanced at him. "O.K.?"

"O.K." Ted unzipped the front of his jacket and pulled out a folded sheet of paper and a weighted leather sap. He handed the paper to James. "That's the one of the church Duke wanted; better give it him afterward."

James took the drawing. "No trouble?"

"No. Dead an' alive hole, whole place was dark, everybody asleep. All except our old bird—she'd been out somewhere. Came in while I was there." Ted grinned. "I bopped her on the daisy from behind just as she was going to turn on the light." He waggled the sap. "Got a lovely spring in it. She'd only got a scarf thing over her head and I gave it her so hard it flipped right back and I nearly dropped it. If she ever comes round she won't worry anybody for a month or two." He jerked his thumb upward. "All in?"

James nodded. Evelyn stopped in his pacing and stood over them. He looked down at the dice.

"They shared my garments among them and cast lots for my clothing."

The other young man rocked back on his heels. "What's biting you, pop?"

The actor turned away. "Bah, ignorant puppies. You know not what you mock."

James stood. "I know one thing. It's about time we sent you up. Come on." He scooped a goat's mask from the floor and threw it to Evelyn. "Get your face on and stand on the platform."

Ted pulled a box into position and stood on it ready to slide the bolt to the trap. The other young man took hold of the winch handle. He eyed the black-robed, goat-headed figure with derision.

"Pleasure to send you up any time, pop. No effort at all."

Really. Police work. So strange. One had, of course, understood that the police needed great patience, but one had not, until now, fully appreciated how much of their time was spent in waiting about. And in such odd places. Miss Seeton stared about her trying to penetrate the almost total darkness of the church interior. She did so hope that she would be able to do whatever it was they wanted her to, though, to be frank, she still wasn't clear—well, not entirely—quite what that was. Admittedly that nice Mr. Foxon—so very sympathetic—had explained it all again, but even he did not appear fully to understand that it was not possible to get an impression, or make a drawing, in the dark, of a church that one had not seen, when one was too, and so was it. In the dark, that was. And although this coat, which Mr. Foxon had so thoughtfully borrowed, was comforting, even if a little large, there were one's ankles. Such a draft. Miss Seeton surreptitiously began to draw her feet up under the blue melton cloth. If one was going to sit here, one might as well utilize the time. She'd do her breathing exercises. She pulled her right foot up onto her left thigh, then reaching down, she grasped her left foot and placed it upon her right thigh. There. That was better. It really was quite extraordinary. When she had originally seen a photograph in *Yoga and Younger Every Day* of a gentleman in the lotus position, it had never occurred to her that she herself might achieve such a contortion. But now she found it comfortable. And, of course, it would, in this instance, warm her feet. Miss Seeton expelled her breath, contracted her stomach muscles and started to inhale. First the diaphragm for a count of five. Then the chest. Then lift the shoulders for a full expansion on the last count. She raised her shoulders for a full expansion on the last count and the maneuver tipped the hood of the coat down over her hat to the level of her brows. Wasn't there …? Yes, surely, there was some light in the body of the church. Miss Seeton peered beneath the hood at a glow showing through the tapestry in front of her. It seemed so yellow. Not like moonlight at all. Probably the effect of stained glass. And, if one were fanciful, one could almost believe that one could hear movement, whispering.

To the congregation who had come up from the crypt and quietly taken their places on either side of the nave, the effect of Duke's innovation was truly magical. They sat in their pews under the wavering flare of four tall black candles and stared in fascination as a dim phosphorescence appeared in the sanctuary, while from the center of it the Devil their master grew slowly from the floor. Bewitched by their own credulity, many of them fell forward on their knees in reverence. They watched the phosphorescence die and saw the shadowy presence of their deity turn and mount the altar steps. A flame was kindled and the light from a black candle on the altar threw his figure into silhouette. Tall, dark, the menace of the curved horns towering above the shaggy head, he moved across in majesty.

Miss Seeton sensed a definite movement on her left. A faint click, a flash of flame and more light grew behind her. She tried to turn her head against the confining hood. With one eye she saw ... ood gracious. A gentleman in fancy dress lighting a candle on the altar.

Opposite the center of the altar, before the brass glitter of the inverted cross, His Satanic Majesty threw up his hands and jerked backward.

The Ashford Division were chronically short of staff. Foxon had been on late duty three nights in succession. Huddled in his overcoat on his three-and-a-propped-legged stool, his spirit was willing but the flesh had betrayed him. He awoke to find the scene before him changed. Where there had been darkness there was candlelight. Where Miss Seeton had been settled on a stool, a hooded pixie now sat cushioned on the air, while beyond the gnome a goat in a black nightdress appeared to see the elf and to throw up human hands. Was this a dream? The Nuscience meeting and the church combined? Where was he? Above all, where was she? He must protect ... His duty lay ... He started to his feet. He only started. The propped leg of the stool was unprepared for sudden action and fell forward; so did he and, throwing out his hands to save himself, he clutched the tapestry.

At his entrance onto the sanctuary stage, the demon king in a dawdling pantomime, Evelyn could feel the grip, knew that he held his audience in a spell. With perfect timing he moved to the high altar, a kingly hand outstretched. A candle blazed, illumining his performance as he crossed to the center—illuminating a parody of human sacrifice. Upon the altar, in miniature, lay the body of a girl: the turquoise cloak widespread, the leaf-green dress slashed down the middle and thrown back to reveal the corpse, marked with an inverted cross in red, the gashed throat allowing the head to loll in an aureole of red-gold hair. The royal progress halted, the goat's head reared up with a strangled bleat and for the first time on any stage Hilary Evelyn played a scene unscripted, unrehearsed. Hands thrust before him to avert the omen—Macbeth before Banquo's ghost—he backed in terror down the sanctuary steps, when a sighing sound as old dust-laden material collapsed made him raise shocked eyes. Above him in a golden dust-specked haze floated a cross-legged figure in a pointed hood. His superstitious drink-sodden brain confused his recent researches into mythology and comparative religions with his earlier professional study of the Bard. Pan—Puck? Puck—Pan? They both began with P and both in their different days had broken the sound barrier for speed.

"Pan," he cried through the enveloping goat's mask. "Pan—the great god Pan." Abject, he bowed his head and struck it on the steps, which made a deep depression in the mask.

"Pan." "It's Pan." "The god." "It's Pan himself." "It's Pan." The congregation took up the cry, some falling forward in obeisance, others, more frightened, starting back.

Foxon knew from the sounds that they were heavily outnumbered and, horrified at what he had done in leaving Miss Seeton to sit revealed, cudgeled his brains for a way out of their predicament. She had 'em awestruck for the moment—so he stayed behind the pillar. But once they rumbled her there'd be a lynching party; they wouldn't dare let her escape. He was prepared to sell his life in her defense, but could one man save her against the odds? Frighten them more, he pleaded silently. Say something—anything—magical, he prayed. Anything to get them on the run. His prayer was answered. The hood lifted.

"*Pan ho megas tethnéke,*" remarked Miss Seeton. Really, what an extraordinary thing to say. Where had she …? Puzzled, she repeated to herself aloud: "*Pan ho megas tethnéke.*" Oh, of course. She remembered now. The voice from the East in Pilate's wife's dream. So like those word association games one sometimes played in class. She could not now be sure quite what the words meant—Roman, she supposed, or Hebrew—but she did remember that that was what the voice had said. And Pontius Pilate's wife was most upset by it.

So were the members of the cult. The godhead, caparisoned on the air, admitted to his name and spoke in a strange tongue.

Miss Seeton peered into the dimly lit church. A lot of ladies wearing masks. And all the gentlemen in fancy dress—like animals. So this was what they had been waiting for. No, no,

Mr. Foxon hadn't made it clear. Surely it was hardly suitable, and one's impression, to be quite frank, was that the whole thing seemed—in a church—well, just a little rude. And, of course, sitting here in front of them like this—so embarrassing. Preparatory to standing up, Miss Seeton began to push her feet down off her thighs, which made the coat bulge in small upheavals.

Behind the assembly a distant rhythm pulsed, vibrating on the senses. The rhythm grew, defined itself as voices singing to a martial beat. Before them the dark vesture of the godhead shifted and ballooned as he made ready to swoop down on them. A woman screamed and ran for the church doors. Great Pan had been invoked and in spite of Miss Seeton's repeated assurance, in poorly pronounced Greek, "Great Pan is dead," the ancient god had roused himself in answer to the call and panic now ensued. The woman who had screamed reached the doors, dragged them wide and ran into the dark. The rhythmic chanting became distinct; the words were clear, were coming nearer.

> "... Christian so-oljer-ers,
> Marching as to-o war ..."

Caught between the older tenets and the new, the devil worshipers broke and flight became a rout. They plunged through the doors and headed for the wood. Basil Trenthorne's trick of sacrificing the doll to keep the Master on his toes had been successful. Holding his black robe well above his knees, his trousered legs high-stepping and all majestic dignity forgotten, His Goathead bounded after his late idolizers.

> "... going on before ..."

The vicar led, Miss Treeves kept pace with him, and behind them Mr. Welsted the draper, acting choirmaster, was followed by the choir in cassocks and surplices. After them straggled clusters of villagers, while Mrs. Blaine, Miss Nuttel and their deputation, now that it came to the point, were prudently backing the vicar from the rear. All mouths were open, voices raised in song; most eyes were lowered to the ground for fear of tripping. Not yet having reached the bend in the path which had floored Foxon, they were approaching the church from the side. A row of windows faced them. The windows …

"Joe—look, Joe—them's lights, isn't they?"

The whisper ran around. The marchers wavered to a stop; the singing faltered. Thrilled to find the Iverhurst ghosts in residence and feeling that numbers were on their side, the choir sang louder and their elders, finding comfort in the noise, followed their lead.

" 'At the sign of triumph,' " they shouted, " 'Satan's legions flee …' "

"Flippin' heck, *look*—they flickin' well do too."

The choirboy's high-pitched excitement silenced them and the villagers stared agape as in the yellow shimmer by the church steps … people? … things? … were visible, moving, running toward the trees, and for one vivid instant they saw a goat, tall, black and in human form, go leaping down the steps in hot pursuit. Some of the bolder spirits made to follow.

"Halt!" barked Sir George. Couldn't have untrained troops followin' the enemy into unknown territory.

The bolder spirits fell back abashed and not unthankful. Not so the dogs. To the canine mind anything that ran meant games. As one, the village dogs broke ranks. Those with leashes slipped them or trailed them and, led by old Mother Dawkin's peke, amid pleas of "Dozey, come back," and "Down, sir—sit," in full yap and cry they streamed into the wood.

The woman's scream had alerted those in the cave below and the sounds that followed presaged trouble. Leaving the other young man by the winch, James and Ted hurried up through the crypt. They peered cautiously. The body of the church was empty, with four black candles still alight. Edging forward, they saw in the sanctuary, outlined by the flame of a single candle on the altar, an ebon figure in a monk's cowl. Ted's scalp prickled. He'd known it: Other Powers. James shone his flashlight. The cowl lifted and Miss Seeton smiled, embarrassed and uncertain. It *couldn't* be—he'd bopped her. A ghost. Ted's stomach had severed its connections and was fluttering free. James, less superstitious and more practical, was listening. The retreating sounds as the village pack went hunting, the voices of the Christian soldiers debating their next move, turned his attention to the open doors. He ran and barred them. He returned, pulled Ted around and shook him.

"Get her," he whispered. "Quick. People outside. I'll wind the platform down and close the crypt. Get back soon as you can."

Ted rallied. There'd been some mistake. He slipped the thong of his sap over his wrist. There'd be no mistake this time. Flexing the sap in his hand, he spun about. From the altar still shone the single candle. The dark-cowled figure was gone.

Foxon, thankful for the enemy's flight and reassured by the singing outside, had decided it was time to leave when the two figures, creeping from the shadows at the far end near the entrance, gave him pause. The shining of the flashlight upon Miss Seeton and the closing of the doors made up his mind. He grabbed her arm and whisked her through the door in the wall behind him. Using her little flashlight, he looked for a way out. There was none. A small, square stone tower. Before him a huge bell squatted on the floor, another, smaller bell beside it, like mother and child in some grotesquery. Near the smaller bell a ladder stood. He aimed the light upward: the ladder disappeared into a gloom the thin beam could not penetrate. The bell tower. The floor space almost covered by the bells, no room to maneuver, no hiding place. Where could he ...? He urged Miss Seeton toward the ladder.

"Can you get up there?" he breathed.

To sit in the dark in drafts. Then all those very old people in fancy costumes. And now to climb? "But why, Mr. Foxon?" she asked reasonably. "Surely we've seen enough."

"Too much," he answered grimly. "We'd an idea something like this might be going on, but never thought they'd be back. That's why we wanted you here, in case you got a reaction that'd give us a line to go on."

"A reaction?" Miss Seeton was bewildered. "I? But how could I ...?"

"I'll explain later—there's no time. Those two in the church're bound to find us here—and they won't let us get away with it; they daren't, they don't know how much we know. Of all the infernal luck, they pick tonight. The people who were singing outside—" He hurried on as she was about

126

to speak. "I don't know who they are but it must be a rival lot since it was hymns. They may bust in but we can't bank on it, and it's no good our yelling, they won't hear." He put his hand on the ladder. "If you could get up there to the top there'll be a maintenance platform where the bells used to hang and louvers in each wall for the sound. You could lean out and attract attention—it's the only chance I can see. I'll stay here and deal with those two but I can't risk a fight till you're out of reach."

"I don't know." Miss Seeton pushed the coat hood back and tried to readjust her hat. "I can't remember ever being on a ladder." She hung her handbag upon one arm, her umbrella upon the other, and stepped onto the first rung. She stepped off it, freed her foot from the coat, collected up the material as best she could and tried again.

Foxon grasped her arm. "Good girl," he whispered. "And good luck. 'Fraid it'll have to be in the dark or they'll see what we're up to." He moved away swiftly, switched off the flashlight, dropped it in his pocket and crouched beside the door.

When Ted came in he came in with a rush, showing for one instant against the light. Foxon jumped him. Ted, who had scoured the sanctuary and found the only other exit bolted on the inside, was prepared for the attack. He twisted as he fell and they grappled in silence. Ted got a hold on Foxon's hair, found an eye with his thumb and gouged. A lucky blow on Ted's bruised nose saved Foxon's sight. Involuntarily Ted, through pain, relaxed his grip and Foxon sprang clear. The spring was his downfall. The side of the big bell gave no foothold and he landed on his head, half stunned. Groping, Ted found his opponent's face with one hand, raised his sap with the other and brought it down. He stood and produced his flashlight. He cast around him, then, seeing the ladder, he flicked the beam up and there, some twenty feet above him, climbed Miss Seeton. Ramming the flashlight, bulb upward, into his breast pocket, Ted leaped forward and went after her.

Chapter 12

Sergeant Ranger was uneasy. During dinner with his prospective in-laws he had learned of the village's latest frolic, the exorcism service. Dinner over, he had telephoned the Ashford police. Brinton was at home and the inspector in charge could see no reason to disturb him. Either way, he pointed out, no harm could come to Miss Seeton. Foxon would look after her. With the fuss there'd been with finding traces of fires around the Iverhurst graveyard, whoever'd been mucking about there would keep well clear and if she and Foxon did meet up with the village jamboree, what harm? The sergeant had to admit the logic, but then this inspector didn't know Miss Seeton. She was quite capable of conjuring a nestful of hornets out of one of her very off hats with a single pass of her umbrella. The whole idea was pretty off anyway. Put Miss Seeton in a church at night—Foxon or no Foxon—and it was a dead cert the whole thing would end up bees-over-titifolah. The Oracle should've put his foot down from the start.

Bob took his reluctant leave of Anne at half past eleven and walked back to the George and Dragon. The village struck him as sinister, without sound or light. Outside

Sweetbriars he stopped, still worried. On impulse he pushed the gate and walked up to the cottage. The door was open. He gathered himself, snapped on the passage light and charged, swerving into the sitting room and flicking down the switch. He nearly tripped over the body. Aunt Em. He knelt down, gently turned her—and sighed with relief. It was that funny old girl who hissed—what was her name, Miss Hicks?—something like that. Anyway there was a pulse and she was breathing. He took off his overcoat and tucked it around her, crossed the room, snatched the telephone receiver and got Dr. Knight, who said that he would come at once. Bob then rang Ashford and reported; adding that the drawers of the writing desk had been dumped out and there were papers all over the floor. Ashford promised to send a patrol car immediately and finally agreed to divert another car to Iverhurst, just in case.

Dr. Knight, on arrival, removed his patient's head scarf and the daisy hat. He examined the scalp. Not, he judged, serious. He'd run her back to the nursing home. He prodded the pompon on the hat. If it hadn't been for that, he opined, it'd've been to the mortuary. Bob lifted Miss Wicks with care. Her eyes opened and she stared at him hazily.

"You struck me senseless," she accused.

While they were stowing Miss Wicks into the car, P.C. Potter, alerted by radio, puttered up on his Velocette. He would stand guard until the squad car came. Accurately guessing what Bob would want to do, Anne had followed her father in her car and was waiting. With a grin of appreciation Bob climbed in and the two of them set off for Iverhurst.

The ladder jolted, then swayed. Miss Seeton clung. Surely Mr. Foxon should have waited until she had reached the top.

With two people on the ladder it was dangerous. And Mr. Foxon was being so … Oh. That was if it *was* Mr. Foxon. Surely he would have spoken. She tried to look down but found that she could not see directly beneath her: only a light coming up and growing brighter. But at least, now that she could, in fact, see, she realized that she was nearly there: the platform Mr. Foxon had spoken of was only just above her. She attempted to reach the next rung; but failed. Try as she would she could not raise her arms. She had climbed up the inside of Mrs. Potter's coat. Miss Seeton was cross. Oh, dash the thing—this was really quite impossible. She let go with her left hand and fumbled with the button loops, managed to undo them and pulled her right arm free, dislodging her umbrella.

"Oh—mind!" exclaimed Miss Seeton.

Like a spear the pointed ferrule aimed for Ted's head, made contact; the umbrella tilted and its handle hooked a rung. It hung awaiting its next chance. This unexpected harpoon made Ted clutch wildly at the air above him; upset his balance. He flung himself back against the ladder and the umbrella handle, accurate with practice, caught him on the nose. He swore.

Oh. It certainly *wasn't* Mr. Foxon. She must hurry.

Sir George was marshaling his troops. Choosing the most trustworthy among the men, he posted guards at both doors of the church. Intrigued, the main section of the villagers converged to watch, to criticize, to supervise. They were ordered back: old men, women and children's places were in the rear. To keep them in their allotted place Sir George suggested that they should carry on: done a good job with their bit of singing; got the enemy on the run. Never knew—might still be a few lurking inside; a bit more caterwauling should flush 'em out. Nigel and young Hosigg, the farm foreman, were detailed to lead the raiding party. Boosted on friendly shoulders, they climbed through the broken windows, calling back, "No enemy in sight." While reinforcements followed them they deployed, unbarred and opened both the doors. The reserve troops jostled in: they peered and pried, they oohed and aahed; one farmhand mounted the pulpit steps, which thereupon collapsed. Nigel meanwhile explored the chancel, moved to the altar. He stood there shocked, then bent down and, lifting the rotting altar cloth, shrouded the puppet's body. He remained for a moment, swallowing; swallowing. He went to fetch his father.

Miss Seeton had just managed to free her other arm when an extra jolt forced her to snatch a hold upon a rung and lose her hold upon her bag.

"Oh, please—mind out!" she called, dismayed.

What was that hellcat throwing now? Ted tilted back his head and the handbag hit his upturned face. He let out a howl of rage and, spurred by pain, flung himself upward. He'd get her for that or die for it. Miss Seeton reached the platform, tried to step off, and the bucking ladder threw her to her knees against the wall. Ted laughed; only a few more feet—he had her. The duffel coat came to him, spreading as it fell, sleeves outheld for the dance. Blinded and breathless, he wrestled with his new encumbrance, but the ladder, as though in shedding itself of Miss Seeton's weight it had also shed responsibility, teetered upright, swayed, seemed undecided, then, leaning over, gathered speed and smacked the opposite wall. With a rending crack of splitting wood, the top half broke; in breaking, broke his hold. The coat released him: Ted shrieked as by the light of his own flashlight he trod his last *pas seul* on air and the coat that had been Death's dancing partner followed him.

Ted's howl of rage, muffled by distance and the door, echoed eerily round the church. Sir George's army halted. Some troops deserted. The stouter hearts closed ranks and held a consultation.

"Cor, that made un jump."

"Where'd be coum from?"

"B'ain't nowhere."

"None but t' old belfry."

"No bat that weren't."

In a body they trepidated toward the bell tower door. Before they reached it, a cracking sound, a shriek which, starting in the sky, came plummeting toward them in crescendo, a thud which shook the floor. They backed aghast. Nigel, returning with Sir George, joined with young Hosigg and they rushed the door. A flashlight showed them the squatting bells, two men's bodies, a splintered ladder, a spilled handbag, an empty coat and lying to one side a silk umbrella, broken. A handbag … umbrella? With dismal misgiving they looked again. There was no more to see.

Outside the church the rear guard felt inspired. It was too clear that Things were Going On. The Devil's hosts were in that church and who, they would like to ask, had got them out? They had. And whose idea was it? they asked again. No one but theirs. Sir George was right. The thing must be finished, properly. They urged the vicar on, they egged the choir, and lifted voices in "Jerusalem."

"… me my spear. O clouds, u-unfold," they implored.

It was a night for prayer: all suits were granted. Dutifully the clouds parted and in strained moonlight the outline of the church took shape: the roof, the battlements, the gargoyled gutters; the bell tower loomed, with gargoyles on each corner.... Each ... corner? Mrs. Blaine squeaked in shock, Miss Nuttel cowered, all craned their necks to look and saw an extra gargoyle nestling there. Their song was dead; their martial spirit quenched. It was the vicar's turn. Deeply impressed by what had taken place and humbly aware that God had shown His hand and blessed their enterprise, he knew his path was clear. It was his bounden duty, and he realized it, to end this desecration of an anointed house. Boldly he stepped forward under His protection to confront this monstrous Impiety aloft.

"Begone!" he cried. His voice and courage gathered strength. "I command thee, unclean spirit." He was stern. "You leave this place and return to your Infernal Home below where thou shalt burn in everlasting fire." Slowly the gargoyle's head was turned toward them. All shrank. They could see the rolling, flaming eyeballs, the forked tongue darting back and forth. The Reverend Arthur braced himself. "Begone, I say, cursed spirit. Come down at once. Avaunt."

The scene was bathed in light as two cars reached the lichen gate. Uniforms jumped from one, Bob Ranger from the other, in time to catch Impiety's refusal.

"I'm so sorry, Mr. Treeves," Miss Seeton called. "I can't come down—I'm stuck."

Chapter 13

The Yard was now officially in charge and Delphick, installed once more at the George and Dragon, which, on this his third visit, was beginning to feel like home, had the passing thought that in view of Miss Seeton's recent history and her unfailing aptitude for becoming the eye of any whirlwind that offered, it might be simpler in the long run now that she was accredited to the force for the authorities to enlarge Plummergen Police Station, of which the normal complement was PC. Potter, Mrs. Potter, Amelia Potter, aged three, and a cat named Tibs, and install a Seeton posse, complete with a mobile unit, who could be on permanent call to assist in her exploits when and where they occurred. What, he wondered, had she got on to now? That the Nuscientists would have been glad to have seen her notes of the meeting was understandable, but they must have known, when the initial attempt failed, that a second try would be too late. Nothing that he could think of—nothing, apparently, that she could think of—explained two vicious attacks upon her life in one night. Conceivably the second attempt could have been due to resentment on the part of the devil worshipers at the penetration of their mysteries by an outsider. Conceivably.

But only just. There must be more to it than that, since to kill for such a trivial reason was extreme to the point of absurdity. Also Foxon, now recovered and suffering only from a slight concussion, suspected that, in the brief glimpse he had had of him down the length of the ill-lit church, his assailant was one of the toughs who had thrown him out of the Maidstone meeting. Certainly the body, on which they had as yet no identification, had worn a black plastic ring, which would seem to place him in Nuscience. Could this be taken as proof of a link between the two rackets? He had interviewed Miss Wicks; but there was nothing helpful in a sibilation concerning the Queen and the Ace of Spades associated with a sense of menace in Miss Seeton's house. Such flummery could hardly be adduced as concrete evidence of ill intent, even against astral powers. Fortunately Miss Seeton's ambience appeared to extend to her friends. Due to her hat, Miss Wicks, now installed in Knight's nursing home and peeping above banks of flowers and fruit and homemade jellies, was having the time of her life instead of her death and whistling out her story to a constant stream of visitors. She had even achieved a paragraph with headings in the local paper, but since she had suffered only violence with neither robbery nor rape she had not attained the nationals. There must have been something someone wanted at Sweetbriars. Something they knew was there. And since only the drawers of the bureau had been searched, they must have found it. Delphick tried again.

"Are you certain," he asked, "that there's nothing missing? A paper of some kind would be most likely from a desk. One of your sketches perhaps?"

Miss Seeton, kneeling on the floor with her portfolio, spread her hands. "It's very difficult, Superintendent, to be sure. So many of the sketches are just notes—and one forgets. But I've been right through them and I can't find anything that isn't there."

Delphick frowned. "Nothing that you've drawn recently? Nothing about any recent drawing that has struck you as odd in any way?"

Miss Seeton looked helpless. "Why, no. Nothing at all. Oh." Memory nudged her. "Nothing, that is, of course, except the church."

"What church?"

"I've no idea. It must have been some church that I'd seen sometime, and wanted to remember, and made a note of. And then didn't. Remember it, I mean."

The sergeant shut his notebook. She was back on form—or rather off. The Oracle generally seemed to be able to toe the ball and follow through, but for himself it was no good taking shorthand notes in English of speech in double Dutch.

"And then," Miss Seeton remembered, "there was that watercolor done by the sea; just to give one something to judge the children's competition by."

"And where is that?"

"I don't know," she confessed. "I'm afraid I lost it—so very careless—and had to do another."

"I see." The superintendent paced Miss Seeton's sitting room. "This second one—the copy—may I see that?"

Miss Seeton stood up. "But of course. I'm quite sure Mr. Jessyp wouldn't mind. It's at the school. He was going to pin them all on the classroom wall this morning and mine was to be there just to give an idea of the view that they were aiming at."

They repaired to the school.

Delphick was struck by the standard of work of children up to eleven years of age and surprised to see the composite pictures and the poem. "You mean they can get away with things like this? In my day when we were told to draw, we drew or somebody wanted to know the reason why." "But surely," Miss Seeton protested, "the main point in such a lesson should be teaching them to see."

Miss Seeton's picture, however, was not on exhibition. She looked around and found her folding sketch frame on the teacher's table. She opened it. Oh. She gazed, nonplussed. Beside her Delphick scanned the somber color wash in sepia tones, in grays and black: a church merging into the background of night sky; into a wood which swept down the slope behind and threatened to engulf it. There was a sense of suspended threat: lightning might strike at any moment; thunderbolts might fall.

"Is this," he asked, "the church that had gone missing?" "Yes," said Miss Seeton, and fell silent.

Delphick waited. Really, she thought, how very difficult. She knew that she must be precise. Precision was so important to the police. But how could one be precise about something that one didn't understand? Something that should have been impossible. And something that was, in any case, precisely the opposite to what one had expected. "Well?" he prompted her.

"It's a little difficult," she said finally. "I'm afraid I don't understand." Well, if she didn't, Bob decided, they'd had it. It was bad enough when she knew what she was talking about, but … He moved to look at the painting. Crikey. Bit gloomy. Bats in the belfry and all that sort of thing. Bats in the …? It was that damned church they were at last night. There was the bell tower at the side they'd seen her peeping out of and'd had to send for the fire brigade to get her down. When in hell had she found time to knock off this little effort? "It looks," said Miss Seeton tentatively, "a little like the church Mr. Foxon took me to last night. I'm so relieved to hear that he's all right. But the other young man's accident. Quite dreadful. And I do feel that it might have been, in part, my fault. He was in such a hurry that he made the ladder sway and I'm rather afraid I dropped things."

Delphick repressed a smile. From the evidence he'd say she'd literally bombarded him to death, and a good job too. "When did you do this picture of the church?"

"Oh, but I didn't," she disclaimed. "I've never seen it. The picture, I mean. I mean I can't think how it got here."

The superintendent looked at Miss Seeton carefully: had she, like Foxon, got concussion too? Well—take it step by step. "You say this is the picture of the church which got lost, and now it's turned up again."

"Oh, no, it didn't," she informed him quickly. "Get lost, that is. Because it was never there." Recognizing that this might, perhaps, sound a little involved, she determined to make it clear. "Not the church itself, I mean. That, evidently, must always have been there. But the first, as I remember, was by day. And this one is by night. And, I think, from a different angle. But although it has, as you say, turned up, one could not say 'again,' because it was not there to start with. The picture, I mean."

Delphick blinked. Was it he who'd got concussion? Bob gazed at Miss Seeton with respect. For once the Oracle was up the spout; she'd got him on the run. The facts began to jell in Delphick's mind. Twice she'd drawn, or thought she'd drawn, a seascape. Twice she'd ended up with pictures of a church. Twice, or he missed his guess, she'd caught a forewarning of trouble, and twice, unconsciously, had set it down on paper. He signaled Bob to get his notebook out and settled down to question her. He learned of where she'd been and what she'd done; of her fall—so very careless; and of the tunnel that led down to the seashore. Obviously the Nuscientists thought that Miss Seeton possessed knowledge which was dangerous to them, so maybe the tunnel was important in some way. Or was it just the church, since that must be the drawing that they'd stolen? But how could they have learned about her burrowing underground? And how could they have found out about the drawing of the church? She insisted that on the first occasion she had been alone and that her sketching frame was already closed and her paints and brushes packed before Lady Colveden had called for her. No one, she was sure, could have seen the picture.

"You yourself saw no one? No one at all? No one passed by?"

"No one, Superintendent, there was no one there at all. Except, of course, the girl."

At last. More questioning. She'd seen the girl again at the Nuscience meeting. Had she seen her since? No. She was sure? Quite sure. Though she had the impression that she was staying in the village. Delphick remembered the beauty sitting at a table alone on the far side of the room at breakfast. Fine. He'd soon have her name and start a few inquiries. What connection could the girl have with the church? He ruminated.

"Can you bear to describe again this so-called service at the church last night?"

Miss Seeton's hands began to stray; her mind went blank. "There was nothing, Superintendent, that I haven't told you. There was very little light and it all seemed rather childish. And then, it was so quick. Some woman screamed and they all ran away. I'm sure that Mr. Foxon would be able to give you a better idea than I could."

Delphick wasn't listening. He watched the restless hands. He smiled and got up. Miss Seeton started to rise. He laughed and stopped her. "No you don't, you stay where you are; I've got a job for you. You've got more paper in that sketching thing of yours? Good. And colored pencils?" They found some in a drawer. "I'm going to borrow Mr. Jessyp's telephone and follow up a few lines—among them local knowledge of tunnels, things like that—and I want you to sit here quietly and think about last night. And then if anything occurs to you, no matter what it is or how silly it seems, just get it down on paper." He sat Bob on a bench near the door, behind Miss Seeton, and left the classroom.

Bob sat and waited as quietly as a stomach striking half past lunch allowed. So far as he could judge, Miss Seeton merely sat. If she didn't buck up they'd get no food, the children'd be back for afternoon classes, and they'd look pretty silly sitting stewing here in solemn silence. He watched as she picked up a pencil, toyed with it—and put it down. Then chose another. She made a few tentative passes on the paper. Then, suddenly, she was working, quickly and absorbed. It dawned on him that the Oracle was back in the doorway, watching and waiting. Miss Seeton finished, put down her crayons and sat back reviewing the result. Apparently it displeased. She picked up the paper and was about to tear it when the

Oracle, beside her in two strides, removed the drawing. She became flustered.

"I'm sorry, Superintendent. It's no good. I've got things mixed. I was trying to give some idea of that affair last night, but somehow it looks more like that meeting at Maidstone. I suppose," she concluded, discouraged, "because they both seemed so silly."

Bob looked over his chief's shoulder and chuckled. This was more like it. Better than that other gloomy thing. Quick, sure strokes showed the church interior with its aisle and pews as viewed from the sanctuary. In the foreground, profiled, one lifted hand holding a black candle dripping wax, the other hand pointing an admonitory finger down to regions below, stood the Master from Maidstone. Before him, briefly limned, the congregation milled in attitudes of devotion or of fear. Apart from the Master only two or three had features delineated: a fair-haired girl whom Delphick recognized at once as the breakfast beauty; a displeasing woman with a beaky nose, wearing a twisted turban in garish colors and a young man with eyes set close together. He pointed to the last.

"Who's he?"

Miss Seeton looked. "I don't think it's anybody. At least not intentionally. It's just—a face."

"And her?" Delphick prodded the turban.

She was apologetic. "That, I'm afraid, is some relation of Sir George's. The hat—so unsuitable—stuck in my mind. But that's what I mean," she explained. "It's all mixed up. Neither she, nor that pretty girl, nor the lecturer were there. Everyone wore masks. They were all at that one Mr. Brinton sent me to. The other one, I mean."

Delphick gave credit to Miss Seeton for sincerity, but not for accuracy. It wouldn't stand up in court, but from his experience of her and the way she worked he'd be prepared to take it as read that all four of them had attended the Black Mass last night. Hilary Evelyn was already under observation. The Colvedens' Aunt Bray, he knew, had moved to a hotel in Rye. He wondered briefly whether Sir George suspected her shenanigans. Probably not. A person's nearest—if not in this case dearest—were usually the last to guess. But from what he'd heard of her she sounded just the type to mix a little witchcraft with her Nuscience. People with barren lives—like your hard-headed businessman, always the conman's easiest sell. And the girl—a Mrs. Paynel with an address in London, he had learned from his telephone inquiries—might well repay investigation. He'd get the Yard to check and delve into her background.

The waltz from *The Merry Widow* lilted from the radio. Merilee Paynel laughed in excitement.

"An omen. They're playing my tune."

She took three steps, spun once, whirled twice, her ball dress floating in soft glimmer, and sank to the floor at Nigel's feet. He placed the cloak that he held ready about her shoulders. She came erect in one swift movement, swept to the floor, turned, dropped a full curtsy to Sir George and Lady Colveden, rose with a radiant smile, was gone. Nigel grinned at his parents, saluted them and followed her.

Miss Seeton watched entranced. Her fingers itched to set it down: the grace; the glamor and the gaiety; the swirl of rhythm; the freedom and the color. When she got home she'd try, must really try, to capture that most difficult thing, a vivid mood of movement.

Sir George cleared his throat. "Lovely gel."

"Yes ..." Lady Colveden sounded doubtful. "But she's a little old for Nigel and we don't know anything about her. And why come to stay in a small place like this? Paynel ..." Her eyes widened in question. "Wasn't there a Paynel who drove racing cars? I seem to remember a few years ago something about an accident and he was killed. It was in the papers."

"Not our business. Bit of experience won't hurt Nigel. Boy's growing up."

"He's only nineteen and—" Lady Colveden shrugged it off. "Come along," she told Miss Seeton. "Dinner's all ready. We've only got to dish up."

The Colvedens, who felt that such diversions as hunt balls were best left to the young in wind, had insisted upon Miss Seeton dining with them as a gesture to the village.

The village was a little overfull of gesture. They gesticulated at each other in heated argument over Miss Seeton's latest escapade. Stan Bloomer and Mr. Welsted came to blows. The awe which the exorcism service had inspired, when all had seen—or had they seen?—a host of nightmare demons in full flight before the representatives of rectitude and virtue, had been forgotten in the excitement of gaping at a quite unquestioned Miss Seeton disguised as a gargoyle. She'd polished off two chaps and tried to fly out through t' tower top on 'er brolly. That weren't right—only one bloke dead; t' other were on his pins again. No thanks to 'er. The trouble for her advocates was to explain how she had reached the top. If they accepted the remains of the broken ladder as evidence that she had climbed, then they were left with a picture of a crouching Miss Seeton, umbrella at the ready, poking the two men off it one by one. Those who maintained that she had tried to escape by flight and then got stuck in the opening found confirmation in the fact that she had admitted it. Said she were stuck, didn' she? All'd 'eard 'er, didn' they? And it'd took the Brettenden fire brigade's longest ladder and Wully Boorman, who'd t' best 'ead for heights, t' oick 'er down. The attack upon Miss Wicks showed Miss Seeton in an even more sinister light. Mrs. Blaine retold the too horrifying story of how, by the mere stretching of an arm through a window, she had knocked poor Eric senseless. Now it was all too clear. She had spells which lingered in her cottage to waylay anyone foolhardy enough to venture there. This theory had gained support from the curious circumstance that on the morning after delivering it the Nuts had quit. They had canceled their milk, announcing that they would be away some weeks. No one knew where they had gone and, since they were keeping their destination secret, it was obvious that they had fled in fear of Miss Seeton's wrath to come.

Unexplained absenteeism was also disturbing the police. Upon request the Sussex force had sent a man to Mrs. Trenthorne's hotel at Rye to keep an eye on her, only to find that she had paid her bill and left but had not left a forwarding address. Others, both in Sussex and in Kent, had informed their various police stations that their houses would be empty during their absence for the next few weeks, but none had given their holiday address. The majority had said that they were traveling. When this information percolated, Delphick asked for an additional check to be made. It was then discovered that a number of houses, chiefly in Kent, were closed and their owners absent; again with no explanation. There was nothing to prevent people from taking holidays; nothing to say that they could not take them all at once; but remembering what he had heard from Scotland, where further inquiries had produced no further intelligence, and in view of what Sir George had told him of Aunt Bray's slip about a secret place, the superintendent was concerned. The search for Miss Seeton's tunnel had proved a failure. The coast was known to be honeycombed with them but few had been traced. They had scoured the seashore for the opening she had described but could not find it. She had led them to the spot where she averred that she had fallen, but either her geography was at fault or else the site had been skillfully repaired and camouflaged. Although it seemed improbably far away, they had even searched the church and tested all the flooring, but with no result. If the Nuscientists had a secret place in the neighborhood, the secret was well kept.

After dinner Sir George determined upon walking Miss Seeton home. He noted with amusement but without comment that she had a new umbrella. It was a stout affair, nylon-covered, with a strong steel shaft. It had been delivered at Sweetbriars with a letter of apology from Chief Inspector Brinton for the fiasco at the church. Would she, the chief inspector had asked, use the enclosed as a working model, to be replaced as necessary? Meanwhile he had sent the remains of her silk one with the gold handle, found in the belfry—which Delphick had given her on a previous occasion—to be repaired and it would be returned to her when ready. But he would like to suggest that in future she use it only on such comparatively safe occasions as afternoon tea with friends. Privately the chief inspector considered that such things as safe occasions and Miss Seeton didn't jibe and that in her case afternoon tea at the vicarage was as likely to turn to mayhem as any other venture in which she might indulge. There was also a rider which had surprised Miss Seeton. Though, naturally, one must not take advantage. Would she, Brinton had insisted, indent for hats destroyed in the course of duty; also for clothes, to be cleaned or replaced as needed. Probably, she decided, just Mr. Brinton's rather tart sense of fun.

Sir George bade Miss Seeton good night and waited for a moment after she had closed her door. Hadn't heard a lock or bolt. Still—couldn't interfere: never give orders in another command's barracks. He looked down the Street. Seemed quiet enough. Should be all right, he supposed. He turned to go home. Lovely gel, Mrs.Paynel.BitoldforNigelthough;Megwasright.Still—shouldn't interfere: never drill the men off parade. He walked slowly back to Rytham Hall. Could be all right, he supposed.

Chapter 14

At home Miss Seeton hurried to her desk, took pencils, brushes, watercolors, and settled down to ensnare the effervescence that was Mrs. Paynel: the sweep of line; swift movement; the exhilaration of a smile; the sparkle of a mood. She worked with enthusiasm, at speed and carefree, and knew the jubilation of the artist when intent and execution flow in unison.

Miss Seeton gazed entranced at the picture she had painted. For once, just this once, she had achieved her aim. Merilee Paynel skimmed across the paper, arms outflung, and laughing, in a swirl of chiffon: almost it was possible to visualize her next action as she dipped in curtsy. The picture roused old ambition from long sleep. Could it be, Miss Seeton wondered, that one was at last improving; that one might, perhaps, however humbly, judge oneself to be a true artist? But no. Surely it seemed so very unlikely. At one's age. She studied the painting again, trying impartially to assess its merits. And slowly rapture died. Before her eyes the colors faded, changed; free-running lines stiffened and movement stilled as another, a different picture, was superimposed. The red-gold hair and the likeness of feature remained; but laughter was gone. The eyes downcast, the figure dressed in blue with a turquoise cloak was seated, the arms hung limp, the hands, upturned and empty, rested on the knees: the image of another mood; of sadness and of suffering; a portrait of despair. This was ridiculous. Some trick of the eyes from strain. A sharp reproof for being too self-satisfied. She glanced down. The seated figure mocked her. Miss Seeton got up and moved away. She would not look at it again until she could judge it properly; until this unhappy vision from a tired imagination had disappeared. She went to the kitchen and filled the kettle preparatory to making that solace for all English ills, a cup of tea.

Disappointment awaited Nigel at the hunt ball. The evening had started well. Merilee had been enchanting with his parents, gay on the drive, vivacious at the dance. He had experienced to the full that satisfaction for the male, to be the envy of his set. Every man he knew demanded an introduction; but except in the Paul Jones he had remained her only partner.

During supper at a table for six, Nigel had diverted the company with a description of the exorcism. Flushed with success, he had not noticed that Merilee's response was lukewarm. She had fallen silent, her smile automatic. He capped his story with a witty description of the assault upon Miss Wicks, which gained an uproarious reception. Except from Mrs. Paynel.

For Merilee it was as if a kaleidoscope had turned in her mind. In a flash all the garish, jagged shapes that formed her present mode of life clicked to a pattern; an unattractive illustration; a yardstick by which to measure her descent.

Thought carried her back four years—or was it forty?—remembering ... Remembering happiness. Two years married and in love: in love with life; in love with a new life stirring. Remembering ... To kill all three in an instant between a patch of oil on a roadbend and—She'd never known what the car had hit. With the pride of sharing Peter's life, and through that pride to end his life. The racing trophy that he had won at Brand's Hatch that afternoon carefully stowed behind; he must relax; she would drive them home; prove that she could take the strain for him when needed. To sit by life and laughter; a brief moment of wrestling fear; to sit by death, with laughter gone; laughter that had ended on a gasp as she had lost control; a last gasp; the first gasp of death. Four years. And still she could not, still would not accept. Would it have been easier if people had blamed her? Given her something to fight instead of leaving her to blame herself, to fight herself, alone. Sympathy from the coroner, kindness from Peter's parents. They were to have called the child after Peter's father; Roberta had it been a girl. Understanding everywhere. Except within herself. And so she had set out to escape herself; to escape from all of them; arguing that since her spirit was dead it could not call in question the actions of her body. She slept around.

Meeting Duke casually at a party, she had become as casually his mistress. He had found her useful; a good saleswoman for the witchcraft cult, though on the obverse side, of Nuscience, she had stalled. She would attend an occasional meeting but she would not join them and she and N. shared a mutual antipathy. Now, she sat at supper with five happy extroverts, Nigel's story compelled her to face herself. It was she who had told Duke of Miss Seeton's drawing of the church. It was she who must carry the responsibility for this attack upon an old woman. She had reasoned that her actions were her own, affecting no one. Now suddenly their effect upon others was brought home. Merilee Paynel was being forced to think. Where was she headed? What doing? Nigel, his family, this Miss Wicks, Miss Seeton, the village as a whole: unthinking, innocent people doing no harm. And she, not innocent, doing harm unthinking. Much to which she had shut her eyes was now in squalid view. She was aware that Duke used blackmail, knew that in more than one case it had led to suicide, but had shrugged away the knowledge as no concern of hers. Also there had been accidents. Now, in clearer vision, had they been accidents, or the removal of inconveniences that might prove dangerous? That Duke and N. were ruthless in the pursuit of money she was mindful. Had she sensed, but blinked, the possibility of murder? One thing of which she was certain: she must go back to the village before it was too late. Back? She reflected bitterly. Wasn't time always that much later than you knew? Could one go back? Ever?

Supper over, Merilee pleaded a headache, and asked to leave. Nigel was distressed by the change in her; she looked drawn and pale. Chastened, and feeling that in some way he was to blame, he cut short her apologies and drove her back to the George and Dragon, where she made amends. Kissing him good night, she clung to him, assured him that a night's rest was all she needed and agreed to lunch with him next day. She remained on the sidewalk to wave as, happy once again, he swung the car around and headed for his home.

There was a knock upon the door. Really. How very strange. Surely it was rather late for anyone to call. Miss Seeton hesitated, then, balancing the tea tray on the edge of the small table in the passage, she reached forward and lifted the latch. Good gracious. How extremely odd. Mrs. Paynel. Miss Seeton stared in disbelief. Just when one had been … But no. She wasn't even going to think of that painting again till after she had had a cup of tea. When she came to look at it again she would find, she was quite sure, that it was at least what she had drawn, though almost certainly not, one was afraid, as good as one had hoped, and not what she hadn't. Drawn, that was.

Finally: "May I come in?" requested Merilee.

Miss Seeton, fearing that she was, perhaps, failing in the ebullience expected of a hostess, stepped back embarrassed. The china clinked as the tray tilted. Merilee took it from her. "Of course," apologized Miss Seeton. "Please do. I'm so sorry. If you'll just put it down there"—she gestured toward the sitting room—"I'll fetch another cup." She turned and hurried to the kitchen.

When Miss Seeton came back with the extra cup and plate of cake and biscuits, Merilee Paynel had thrown her cloak over a chair and was seated by the fire, staring, withdrawn. Miss Seeton put on another log, sat down and drew the table toward her.

"I'm so sorry," she apologized again. "I should have asked: I'm afraid it's China and will you have it weak or strong? Sugar? Milk?" The girl came out of her abstraction. Tea was poured; the plate was offered and refused.

"Don't," said Mrs. Paynel abruptly, "ever open your door at night unless you know who's there."

Miss Seeton was surprised. So unusual for the young to offer one advice. Naturally one knew it was well meant. And, doubtless, a very sensible precaution in London, or wherever Mrs. Paynel came from. But evidently she had no idea of village life, where people mostly retired early. And certainly never called upon one late. Unless, of course, the circumstances were unusual. Or it was an emergency. In which case, of course, it would be very wrong not to. After all, Mrs. Paynel herself had called late and she wouldn't have got in if she hadn't. If she hadn't opened the door, that was to say. It struck her how very changed Mrs. Paynel was from the laughing girl who had set out for the dance. Almost a different woman.

This different woman began to speak urgently, blaming herself and trying to persuade her hostess of the danger in which she stood. She made little headway. Told that the attack upon Miss Wicks must have been made by one of the Nuscientist bully boys waiting in the cottage for a chance to murder the owner on her return, Miss Seeton was moved from incredulity to indignation. No one, she pointed out, would have waited for her in the cottage, since she wasn't there. And as for murder: she found the suggestion as melodramatic and distasteful as it was ridiculous. When applied to herself.

"For a detective"—Merilee's comment was dry—"you're remarkably innocent or else you're brilliant."

Miss Seeton was shocked. She, at once, made it quite, quite clear that she was in no way connected with, or not in that way, but only, as it were, attached to—and, even that, in a different way entirely from the way which Mrs. Paynel was suggesting—the police. For the drawing of Identi-Kits, she added to clear any possible obscurity. Asked if she had been drawing Identi-Kits at the church the night before, Miss Seeton was at first confused; then disturbed when her visitor frankly admitted to being there.

Merilee leaned forward and put her barely tasted cup upon the table. "Can one go back?" she asked. "If you've been all kinds of a fool can you go back?"

Miss Seeton considered. Such a difficult question. And not one, one feared, that one had ever thought about. On the whole, she finally decided, one could not. Or, alternatively, if one could, there would, surely, be little advantage since one would only find oneself back at the beginning and ready to make the same mistakes again. Sensing Miss Seeton's dilemma, Merilee got up and moved to sit on the arm of her chair. She smiled down at her.

"Look," she said, "you don't understand me, and I'd certainly got you wrong. But, please, try to believe me when I tell you you're in danger. I know what I'm talking about." She laughed shortly. "For that matter I'd be in danger myself if they knew that I was here trying to warn you."

Danger? Miss Seeton began to worry. Though ridiculous, of course, when referring to oneself, other people did get into difficulties—and even, sometimes, into danger; that one knew. "But do you mean that these people would seriously try to kill you? It seems so—forgive me—so very extreme."

"Nothing's extreme where money's involved. They'd try." She looked down at the empty hands that lay upturned in her lap and shivered. "I'd never've thought I'd mind. I believed that I'd died four years ago in hospital."

Miss Seeton sighed. One did wish that people wouldn't talk in riddles. She moved to take one of the girl's cold hands. "Please, Mrs. Paynel, if it's as you say, wouldn't it be wiser to speak to Superintendent Delphick? You'll find him such an understanding man and I know that he'll do everything he can to help."

154

Merilee looked around the room. This place, this funny little character, Sir George and Lady C... . Nigel. Unconsciously she spoke the last word aloud. She stood. "What odds?" She picked up her cloak and put it on. "As you failed to say: you can't go back."

Miss Seeton rose quickly. "Oh, but—I didn't mean ... Or, rather, that is to say, if I had, I wouldn't have. I suppose, what I really feel is that it wouldn't help, because then one would only be back where one was before. But not in that sense. In the sense of going back, that is to say. One has to—or so I should imagine—always go forward. And anything that has happened in the past: wouldn't that—I don't know—give one a better sense of values and help one, perhaps, make it easier, in some ways, to manage one's life, to understand the future? Like history. Only, of course, that never does, because people don't. Understand, I mean." Miss Seeton, who had never in her life learned from experience and never would, and whose history was bespattered with incidents the majority of which were due to just such a failure in understanding of the past, was understandably doubtful whether she had made herself clear. "I'm so sorry," she apologized. "I'm talking far too much. And not very helpful, I'm afraid."

Merilee looked at her with affection. "I wouldn't say that. I'll talk to your superintendent in the morning. And as to the other—I'm having lunch with Nigel. Who knows? We'll see." She walked to the passage. "Now come along and bolt the front door behind me."

Miss Seeton returned to the sitting room, sat down at the desk and tilted the lampshade to study the painting. It was, as she had half known it would be, a seated portrait of sorrow. It looked, she was forced to acknowledge, so very like Mrs. Paynel when she had sat on the arm of the chair, her hands lying in her lap. But why, she wondered, had she got the colors wrong? Mrs. Paynel's dress was of misted grays and pink and the cloak was a golden velvet. Here the dress was green and the cloak turquoise. There was something curiously familiar about it but she couldn't place it. Was it some painting of a Madonna, some pietà that she had seen at some time and copied quite unconsciously? No such picture came to mind. And yet the familiarity still nagged her. The red-gold hair, the green dress, the turquoise cloak ... No. She couldn't place it.

Still smiling from her encounter with Miss Seeton, Merilee Paynel shut the front garden gate behind her with a squeak and turned right to cross to the George and Dragon. From the shadow of a bush which overgrew the fence two men stepped forward to confront her.

"Keeping strange company, aren't you?" suggested Duke.

Chapter 15

Nigel Colveden was engaged in a heated if one-sided argument: she couldn't, she wouldn't have stood him up; and anyway she'd said she never broke engagements. The landlord of the George and Dragon countered with caution. Young ladies in these days were just as apt to stay out all night as young gentlemen; and that Mrs. Paynel hadn't returned last night was none of his business. Her things were still in her room and she wouldn't thank him for letting the cat out of the bag that she'd spent a night on the tiles. He'd have helped young Mr. Nigel if he could, but he wasn't going to let himself in for libel, defamation or any of that.

Delphick came in for lunch and Nigel appealed to him: Mrs. Paynel was missing, would the police …? The superintendent too felt that Mrs. Paynel's cutting of a lunch date was hardly his affair. On the other hand, her whereabouts, in view of his suspicions of her, were. He questioned the proprietor. Faced with authority, the landlord was cooperative. No, Mrs. Paynel hadn't returned last night and her bed hadn't been slept in. No, she'd said nothing about being away, in fact her car was still in the garage. Mrs. Paynel certainly wasn't in when he'd locked up and gone to bed at midnight, but she had a key and was free to come in any time.

Nigel protested: but she'd been back well before twelve. She'd had a headache and they'd come back early and he'd dropped her at the door. She must, he insisted, have gone into the pub. Delphick pondered. It seemed odd. Where would she have gone at night without a car? To the best of his knowledge she knew no one in the village. He asked Nigel. No, he didn't think she'd met anybody except himself and his parents—and of course Miss Seeton. Miss Seeton? Nigel explained that Miss Seeton had been at the Hall the previous evening before they set out for the dance. Miss Seeton? Delphick reflected. It was Mrs. Paynel who'd seen the first drawing of the church. Had she reported it to someone in Nuscience? He glanced across at Sweetbriars. He could see no reason … It seemed unlikely. Better check. He crossed the Street. Nigel followed.

Miss Seeton, interrupted at lunch, did her best after her own fashion to be helpful. Why, yes, Mrs. Paynel had called on her last night. Had Mrs. Paynel spoken of the church? Miss Seeton glanced at Nigel in embarrassment and then admitted: yes, actually she had. In fact she had said that she had been at the meeting there, which seemed, Miss Seeton added hurriedly, so very unlike her somehow. Had Mrs. Paynel given a reason for her visit?

"Danger," replied Miss Seeton.

Delphick was sharp. "Danger to whom?"

"Well, she did speak of some danger to me, which, as I pointed out, was nonsense. But she did also speak of danger to herself." Miss Seeton stopped, astonished. "But, Superintendent, haven't you seen her yet? She was going to tell you all about it."

"About what?"

"Well, she did mention that she would be in some danger herself if she warned me."

"Of what?" persisted Delphick.

But here Miss Seeton could not help him, since of what she had been warned she was not sure.

"What else did she say?"

Miss Seeton temporized. She was uncertain how much of what had been said Mrs. Paynel would prefer kept confidential. She remembered the question "If you've been all kinds of a fool can you go back?" Which implied, one imagined, that at some time Mrs. Paynel had, perhaps, behaved a little foolishly and had since regretted it. In any case, in front of Nigel, it would be dreadfully wrong to repeat anything that might cause misunderstanding. "Well," she said at last, "Mrs. Paynel spoke of money being involved. Which was why, she said, it would be dangerous."

Nigel's mounting temper could no longer be restrained. This was rubbish. She must have misunderstood completely. To suggest that Merilee was a witch and would have gone to that crazy service …

Delphick cut him short. "Be quiet, Mr. Colveden. We need the truth, whether you like it or not, if we're to get anywhere. Go on," he encouraged her.

Miss Seeton looked hunted. Her glance strayed round the room seeking inspiration, lingered on her desk, then shifted guiltily as she remembered last night's painting. She couldn't—definitely she couldn't. And certainly not with Nigel there. It would be most unfair. "It really would be better if Mrs. Paynel spoke to you herself."

Delphick's mouth was set. "I think we'll have to take it that she can't." How was it that this funny little cuss always seemed to be a jump ahead of everybody without even trying? She was stalling. Why? Because the boy was here? And that conscious-stricken look at her desk meant another sketch, of that he was certain. Maybe that could explain things if she wouldn't. "Come along," he admonished her, "you're hiding something. Which could indeed be dangerous, both for you and for Mrs. Paynel. And any drawing"—he regarded her accusingly—"is now police property." He smiled. "Remember, you're under contract."

With reluctance Miss Seeton rose, moved to the desk, collected the watercolor and handed it to Delphick. "I don't think it can help you, Superintendent; it's so—so different from what I had intended."

Nigel joined them. "But that's the doll," he exclaimed. He stopped. It was also Merilee. A Merilee he hadn't known. But her. Memory pictured the doll as he had last seen it on the altar and the sick feeling he had experienced then returned.

Delphick had been shown the mutilated doll at police headquarters. The doll? "So different from what I had intended?" And Mrs. Paynel had admitted being at the church. He went to the telephone. Brinton was in and agreed to divert the nearest patrol car to Iverhurst church immediately. Delphick rang Bob: to bring the car at once. Nigel ran from the cottage.

Merilee Paynel lay, as had the doll, upon the altar. The golden cloak hung in shadowed folds: over it trailed, still shimmering in destruction, the ball dress, slit from neck to hem. Incongruously the left leg bore a green snakeskin garter. The gashed throat with its congealed bloodfall, the mutilated body with the inverted cross scored into the flesh across the abdomen and up to the sternum—nothing could take from her an earned serenity, the dignity of lasting peace.

Dr. Knight, standby for the county pathologist, who was on holiday, straightened from his examination and Chief Inspector Brinton, who had beaten an ambulance to the church by a short wheel, made his first comment.

"All right, so it's ritual stuff again."

"You think so, Chris? Certainly we're meant to." Delphick moved away to leave matters to the scenes-of-crimes officers.

"What else?" asked Brinton.

Dr. Knight closed his bag and with Sergeant Ranger followed Brinton and Delphick down the aisle. Despite their professional immunity, four very angry men. An altercation started up outside. Recognizing Nigel's voice, Delphick snapped:

"For God's sake keep that boy out of here."

Bob sprinted ahead. Nigel was struggling with the two uniformed men from the patrol car which had been first on the scene. Bob ran up to them.

"All right, let him go."

"Is she …?" gasped Nigel. He gulped and tried again. "Is she …?"

"Please, Mr. Colveden, there's nothing you can do here. If you'll just go home, we'll get in touch as soon as possible."

"What the hell d'you mean, you'll get in touch?" Nigel swerved and darted forward. Bob put out a foot and, as Nigel fell, brought the side of his hand down with exact precision behind the boy's left ear. Gently he laid him on his back. Dr. Knight joined them, knelt and checked the pulse, lifted one eyelid, then opened his bag.

"Coat sleeve," he ordered. Bob eased off Nigel's jacket and rolled up a shirt sleeve. The doctor swabbed, inserted the needle of a hypodermic and pressed the plunger home. "That'll hold him till tomorrow morning. The ambulance can drop him off at his home, since they're not needed; get him to bed and tell his parents that I'll be along to explain."

Above them the superintendent spoke. "You did the best you could, sergeant, but your reactions are getting slow." Bob looked up in surprise, but the Oracle was looking directly at the patrol officers. "You should've been able to catch Mr. Colveden when he stumbled and saved him from hitting his head on that gravestone."

"Don't agree," contradicted Dr. Knight. He too looked straight at the uniformed men. "From what I saw, your sergeant saved him from the worst. He grabbed quickly enough but the boy was twisting as he fell. That's how he hit the back of his head. Don't think there'll be any concussion, but gave him a shot in case of delayed shock."

The car crew appeared stolid. Finally the driver spoke. "Dangerous places, graveyards. Specially all wooded and overgrown like this. Easy enough to trip. Could've been nasty but for the sergeant."

The ambulance got under way, followed by the doctor. Delphick surveyed Nigel's little red M.G. He appraised his sergeant. No, it wouldn't do. Bob could wear it on one foot. He asked one of the mobile unit to return it to Rytham Hall. The Ashford murder squad were left in charge at the church to see what they could find and Brinton, telling his own driver to follow, got in the back with Delphick, leaving Bob to drive.

"Only one garter?" ruminated Brinton. "Could that mean fetish business?"

Delphick was somber. "No, there would only have been the one."

"How come?"

"You should study your subject, Chris. The snakeskin garter's the ancient badge of a witch's rank."

"Well," asked Brinton again, "if not ritual, what else?"

"Silence," replied Delphick. "She was going to talk to me."

"How d'you know?"

"Miss Seeton." Brinton flinched. Delphick relayed his conversation with her.

"She know any more?"

The superintendent shrugged. "I don't think so. She very properly, but unfortunately, told Mrs. Paynel to speak to me."

"So now," reflected Brinton, "they'll go after the Brolly."

"They're bound to. They don't know how much Mrs. Paynel told her. But with the girl dead, Miss Seeton's report of such a conversation could stand up as evidence. And a sworn statement from Miss Seeton herself wouldn't help us, because she doesn't know anything."

Brinton snorted. "And even if you gave it out she'd made one, it wouldn't help her, because, as all chummies know, sworn statements have a way of backfiring in court under a good defense. So all right," he concluded, "I'll put a guard on her round the clock, though with manpower as it is I'll have to invent the men. And," he added bitterly, "we'll be under pressure from now on. No more hope of keeping things quiet; this killing'll fairly stir it up. There'll be a real hoohah."

Chapter 16

Important news must not be kept from the nation. Murder is important. An attractive happening had taken place. It had attracted the newspapers, the television crews and the sentimental general public, ever ready to be appalled by horror provided that it is horrible enough. The setting of Mrs. Paynel's death paraded all the features dear to the public's sympathetic heart. A beautiful girl, naked, decoratively mutilated, with overtones of rape and undertones of sorcery; with true romance in death suggested by the sacrifice upon the altar of a church. Coach tours had been hastily rerouted. After a duty call at Iverhurst, armed with scissors and with knives to cut or hack mementos from the church, a commercial enterprise unsportingly foiled by the police, these modern pilgrims had converged on Plummergen. They besieged the George and Dragon, where the victim had been staying and where she had last been seen alive. Learning of the dance at Maidstone, they had called to offer their condolences at Rytham Hall, but Sir George and Lady Colveden had kept Nigel incommunicado, had padlocked the gates and were using a side entrance with a key. For two whole days the locals basked in reflected glory. They told their stories—"The Brolly in the Belfry" was popular—they appeared in print, on television screens, they pointed to the constable on duty outside Miss Seeton's cottage: could it be house arrest? One enterprising photographer had secured a picture of the crown of Miss Seeton's hat by standing on the roof of his car and shooting over the wall as she knelt weeding in her garden. Then the pressure was relieved by the wife of a well-known Member of Parliament who sued her husband for divorce, citing his nephew as correspondent. This true romance in life suggesting the likelihood of a test case in law had proved irresistible and Plummergen was once more left to its own devices. Somehow these devices lacked their usual zest. The villagers did their best, took sides: they vilified Miss Seeton and each other; aspersions were cast on the police, on Nigel Colveden; dark things were hinted. But the casts produced no rise; hints were but hints; the essential leadership was lacking. Where were the Nuts?

Below Iverhurst church some two hundred expectant disciples of Nuscience awaited with complacency the end of the world; the extermination of their relatives and friends. Meanwhile they prepared themselves to sow the seed of a new civilization, either on this planet or on another, according to their whim or their proficiency in breathing and transportation. The vast main cellar had been discreetly curtained into three partitions: female dormitory, male dormitory and communal living space. Here the devotees, for the most part, sat, practiced their breathing and conversed; did crossword puzzles, played games; they read, or they dreamed; enduring discomfort, iron rations and the unsanitary arrangements below the crypt, cushioned by the recognition of their paramount importance in the world to come.

The lower cave, which led to the tunnels and the exits, was forbidden territory. It was reserved for the hierarchy. Here, it was understood, the Master, attended by his acolytes, Trumpeters and Majordomes, expended his time in prayer. The Majordomes patrolled the upper cellar in rotation, keeping order, encouraging the fearful, settling squabbles, including a sharp disagreement on a question of protocol among Mrs. Trenthorne, Miss Nuttel and Mrs. Blaine.

After the hoohah that the chief inspector had predicted, Delphick and Brinton in the latter's office assessed the position. They knew no more in regard to Mrs. Paynel's murder than they had done at the start. Her parents-in-law had traveled from Gloucester, had formally identified the body and had arranged for her to be buried beside their son. The police inquiries were at a standstill. Everyone closely connected with Nuscience had disappeared and they could get no news of them. In Brinton's view the Nuscientists had scarpered and the police'd just have to wait till they turned up somewhere else. Anyway there was nothing to say that Nuscience was mixed up in it; more like the witch lot from the look of it.

"And," he concluded, "with a killing to account for, they'll all've taken to their brooms. So all right"—he glowered in frustration—"why brooms, for God's sake?"

Delphick grinned. "They didn't—I told you you should check your facts, Chris. Witches mostly rode on sticks with a phallic symbol at one end. The twig skirt to hide the stick's indecency was thought up as camouflage during witch hunt times. But I don't think we'll find any of them have flown far. My guess is they've all gone to ground—literally. And I still maintain Nuscience and the witches are connected."

"You've nothing that says so except your girl friend's doodling."

"That and fact that we know Mrs. Paynel was at a Nuscience meeting, wore a witch's garter and later admitted to being with the witches at the church. And although Foxon can't swear to his attacker, the black plastic ring on the body brings in Nuscience again."

Brinton humphed. "What'd they stand to gain by it all?"

"At least a quarter of a million cash, I should say." Brinton sat up, incredulous. "Think it out, Chris. We've the best part of a couple of hundred people to account for. They'll have all their portable valuables with them and even if we put it at its lowest, say a thousand pounds a head, a couple of hundred thousand's a nice stake and it's more likely four times that. No, I'll swear they're around here somewhere." He leaned forward to pore once again over the maps they had spread upon the desk; maps old and new. With a sigh Brinton returned to comparing distances, calculating, estimating; getting nowhere. "Surely, Chris," Delphick protested, "there must still be people who know at least where some of the old smugglers' routes ran."

"Don't doubt it," returned Brinton. "But the owlers kept their secrets well. Still do, for that. You forget, Oracle, owling was big business round these parts and Romney Marsh the center of it. If the lads couldn't've kept their traps shut there'd've been an end to it."

"And there hasn't been?"

The other shrugged. "All right—from what I hear it still goes on, though half the time these days with human cargo. So what? It's not my pigeon; let Customary Excuses cope with it."

Delphick frowned. It was a thought. He reached for the telephone. It took him nearly an hour to set it up. Customs and Excise finally agreed to have a launch with two Water Guards on day and night patrol to cover the short stretch of coast which Delphick read off from the map. The official reason for their involvement: a tip-off from the police that there was to be an attempt to smuggle currency and jewelry across the Channel. Fortunately there was a small headland where the Guards could lie up by day. By night they would drift in close to keep their watch. Could the superintendent pinpoint the cave he spoke of any nearer? Delphick couldn't. He explained the circumstances. Could the men on the detail have a talk with this Miss Seeton? Delphick objected: he didn't want any activity showing in the district; if his birds caught wind of it they might desert the nest. No need, Customs pointed out, to walk the lady over the ground again. If she couldn't find it, she couldn't find it. But the boys knew the terrain pretty well and a chat with the lady about where she'd been and what she'd been doing when she fell through on the Downs and came out on the shore might clue them in: the shape of a rock; what kind of scrub was growing; the outline of the dunes when she climbed back. Never knew your luck. Didn't do to miss a trick. Delphick was forced to agree. It would take Customs a little while to get things organized. High tide was twenty-two, twenty-five. Did the superintendent know Judy's Gap? He didn't. Go to Rye, he was told, turn left on the road to Camber, straight on and pull up on the verge a mile beyond Camber. If he'd flash a light signal—one long, two short, one long—with the tide the launch could come right in and the lady would only have a small strip of beach to walk across. It was an isolated spot and they'd be able to keep watch on the coast at the same time. Delphick undertook to produce Miss Seeton there at ten-thirty, he'd get over to Plummergen at once and arrange it; though privately he felt that any little chat with MissEss about her doings to somebody unused to her idiom would only clue them in to Colney Hatch. He rang off and got to his feet. He'd get over to Plummergen at once ... Chris might moan about manpower but at least there was this advantage in having put a guard on her: for once he knew exactly where she was and she couldn't go gallivanting off on her own, getting into mischief.

In Miss Seeton's sitting room, after a series of telephone calls around the district, Delphick replaced the receiver. Typical. If you wanted anything kept quiet in this village you'd find even the dogs discussing it at every tree that lined the Street. But need to know something important and nobody knew a thing. Someone must've seen the car which called for her. He'd guarantee had Miss Nuttel or Mrs. Blaine been about they'd've had the make of the car, its number and the driver's life history; it'd all be wrong but at least it would be a starting point. Whereas this oaf ... He looked at the constable who had been on duty at Sweetbriars.

"But you saw the car. You saw the driver. He spoke to you. You saw him go up to the door and speak to Miss Seeton. You saw him come back with her and get into the car. You saw them drive off. Surely to God having seen all that you must remember something."

The constable shuffled his feet. "Well, sir, I remembers it like, but come to that I didn't notice overmuch. He were in uniform and said as he were from H.Q. to fetch her.

The bloke were youngish like and the car were dark—black 'twould be likely—so I says to meself, all right, while she were gone like, I'd get meself a cuppa."

"But you said they went south over the canal. Didn't even that strike you? It's not even in the right direction."

"Well, sir, like it is and it isn't. I doubt but you can get t' Ashford that road—bit long o' course."

Delphick gave it up. Chris had said he'd have to invent the men for this detail. This particular specimen was evidently the product of a tired mind.

A report came through from Ashford: Potter, Plummergen's P.C., on his rounds, had wirelessed to headquarters regarding a black Humber driving at a very fast speed on the road across the Downs. He had turned and followed long enough to get the number, a London registration, before being outdistanced. Told of the hunt for a false police car, he thought it a possible. Had taken it to be chauffeur driven, but the police cap would look the same from a distance. Also had the impression of a passenger in the rear. A message had been circulated to all vehicles on patrol, but no news so far. Delphick planned quickly. If they failed to find Miss Seeton in time, could a car be sent to take Sergeant Ranger to Judy's Gap so that he could explain the situation to the Water Guards? Delphick himself elected to remain in Plummergen. Since the alert for the black Humber had followed immediately on Potter's message and there was no further advice on the car, it was likely in his view that it had been driven off the road somewhere in the vicinity. Could Potter be ordered back to Plummergen so there'd be somebody on standby with a grain of sense? And if they were shorthanded their end they could have Miss Seeton's ex-guard back and welcome. Delphick rang off and unfolded a map.

The road across the Downs led past the church and through Iverhurst to join in London-Hastings road. Iverhurst? They no longer had a man on duty at the church but with all the publicity it had received it was highly improbable … The car might've got through and it seemed logical they'd aim to get her out of the district fast—if she was still alive. Pacing, restless, he came to a halt before the fireplace; found himself staring at the picture above the mantel. A watercolor of a wind-swept moor, a bleak impression of heather and racing clouds. A gray day. Bob, in a flash of inspiration, had once told him that it was Miss Seeton's portrait of him. The strained lines of Delphick's mouth relaxed for a moment. Could be Bob'd been right: could be she was right. He felt bleak enough. Gray enough. He blamed himself for ever allowing her to become involved in police work; reproached himself for failing to provide adequate security. Innocence didn't belong in this game and well he knew it. He'd guessed this crew would be ruthless and the killing of Mrs. Paynel had shown they wasted no time. If the Humber was to be found, the patrols were the best bet. Nothing was to be gained by his running round in futile circles. So the superintendent settled himself with what patience he could muster to wait for news. It'd been a clever trick to send a decoy police car to fetch her. Even someone less trusting than Miss Seeton would never have thought to question it.

Really, wondered Miss Seeton, weren't they, perhaps, going just a little fast? One had always looked upon the police as such very careful drivers. But then, again, one was inclined to forget that they had to be prepared for emergencies. Which would mean, of course, that they would need to become accustomed. And probably didn't notice it. Speed, that was.

The car careened around a corner and Miss Seeton held on to the strap that hung between the windows beside her to save herself from being thrown across the seat. Certainly the young man did seem to be in a great hurry. Perhaps Mr. Brinton had told him to. Though, of course, to be precise, he had not mentioned the chief inspector by name. He had merely said that he was from police headquarters at Ashford. So that one had presumed ... But, in fact, one supposed that he could possibly have been referring to the superintendent. But no—somehow his sudden, unexpected arrival, and the rush, was something that one associated more with Mr. Brinton than with Superintendent Delphick, who was always so very calm and had everything so very well organized. She did wish, she must admit, that he had made it a little more clear quite what it was they wanted her to do. She looked toward the driver; only the shoulders in the uniform jacket and the peaked cap were visible outlined in the faint light from the dashboard. So very young, surely—hardly more than a boy—to be a policeman. Miss Seeton smiled. They always said that as one grew older they always were. He had said that they needed her to identify someone, but he certainly had not explained whom it was they expected her to identify. Or even where. He had mentioned something about a wood. Which seemed, when one thought of it, such a very odd place to choose. But one really didn't like to ask too many questions. Or, at all events, not at this speed. And on such a winding road. Though, fortunately, there didn't appear to be much other traffic. Only a policeman in uniform on a sort of motor scooter. Actually he had turned round after them. She had quite thought, for a moment, that he was going to join them. Or, possibly, stop them. But no.

He'd only followed them for a moment or two. No doubt he'd recognized the police car.

The car turned off the road, ran a short distance over uneven ground and pulled up under some trees. The young man jumped out and opened the rear door. By the dome light Miss Seeton saw his face more clearly than she had at the door of her cottage when he called for her. There was something vaguely familiar … But no. She felt sure she'd never seen him before. Unless, of course, she'd noticed him at Ashford police station sometime, without really noticing him, so to speak. How very unfair it was, on consideration, to associate close-set eyes with a shifty or unstable character. People couldn't help their physical attributes. It was simply prejudice. And, in any case, naturally, he wouldn't be in the police force if he were.

The driver touched the peak of his cap.

"If you'll follow me, miss," said Basil Trenthorne.

Chapter 17

Miss Seeton followed the light and the blue serge trousers. The young man still appeared to be in a hurry. At least the track was fairly clear, though she was glad of her umbrella to ward off stray brambles that whipped back at her from his passing. It was something of a relief when at length her conductor slowed. Ahead of them a glow showed through the trees: they had come to the edge of a small clearing. He signaled her to stop and switched off his flashlight. Obediently Miss Seeton waited.

"Hang on where you are for a minute, miss," he whispered, "while I put on my disguise. Never do to go up there in the uniform." He sniggered. "Scare the craps out of 'em." He moved away and was hidden by the dense undergrowth at the side of the track they had followed.

Up there? Miss Seeton peered round the trunk of a tree. Light was flickering from flambeaux set in rings on stakes driven into the ground. There was a lot of smoke with the wavery flames. Didn't they use heavy wicks set in tar? Or was it oil? She couldn't remember. That would account for the smell, which at first she'd taken to be paraffin. But then, of course, paraffin was an oil, in one sense, so, perhaps, that was, after all, what it was. In front of her was a rough square platform. It must be nearly three feet high and at least double that in width, she judged, made of branches which, one supposed, would have been cut from the trees around. She could hear voices and laughter but could see no one, nor could she distinguish words. They must, whoever they were, be on the far side of that sort of platform thing. The whole effect was rather eerie and, if one were fanciful, which, thank heaven, one was not, it would have been easy to imagine a stake rising from the middle of the structure with Joan of Arc lashed to it while the English soldiery caroused.

Who could they be? And what could they be doing here so late at night? And what had it to do with the police? One did hope that it wasn't those silly people in masks again. And if it was, how could one possibly be expected to identify anyone? Especially when it was so dim and smoky. No doubt the young man would be back in a moment to explain. One was, of course, naturally, quite sure that, being in the police, he was a most estimable character. But, if one were honest, there was no denying that he did not give one quite the same feeling of confidence as did, for instance, the sergeant. Or even that nice ebullient young Mr. Foxon.

Basil Trenthorne pulled off his cap and knelt to retrieve the parcel he had concealed beneath a bush earlier that evening. This was it. This was where he'd show them—James and the others, who'd been riding him all afternoon because he wouldn't chop branches and help to get the stage set up. Little they knew. Who'd tagged the final touches and really set it up after those dumbsters had finished tying the branches in place, fixed the torches and gone back by the Downs entrance to put in an appearance at the cave? The cave. The thought of his mother down there waiting for the end of this world and imagining she'd be at least President of the next made him chuckle. He'd thought once or twice of telling her he knew she was a witch. That'd've cut her down to size. Glad he hadn't. He'd make more out of it this way. He didn't know how much she'd taken with her to the cellar—she wouldn't tell him—but he did know she'd drawn plenty from the bank. And all her jewelry. She could kiss that lot good-bye. No more thinking up tricks to get money out of her. Duke and N. had promised him the whole of her cough-in plus a bonus for tonight's job. He looked at his watch. He'd timed it pretty well but—he lit a cigarette—better give it a few minutes yet. He took a drag. Those who thought smoking pot was off the curve weren't on the wire; weren't in view at all. It just put your mind in gear and made you see where you were going. And if that old sock was catching cold waiting for him, let her worry. He'd soon warm her up. Ted'd made a proper rib of putting her off the map. Well, if Ted was burning down there now in hell-fire where she'd sent him, she'd soon be roasting right alongside. He took another pull, blew smoke and laughed. Most of the staff, 'specially old Evelyn, were hopping at being kept hanging about so long. Usually Duke and N. switched the money box, then got out, and the rest scattered three days or so after the gulls were settled in their Secret Nest. But this time, with the busies around testing the church floor and God knows what, they'd been forced to wait. Granted the gang could always slip in and out of the Downs entrance, but Duke'd said not more than two at a time—till today—in case they were noticed. Normally any local bobbies should've chucked in before this—even with Duke sticking Merilee on the altar to copy the doll—but a superintendent from the Yard and this wretched old woman were something they hadn't bargained for. So now Duke insisted on all this witchery in the wood to draw their attention before he'd move. Basil checked his watch again. 'Bout a minute to go. It was only a mile to the sea through the tunnel but carrying the loot could slow them up a bit. And then they had to get the box on board the boat. Old Evelyn and his lot should be halfway to the Downs exit. Anyway they had to take their timing from him and not start their cars till the fire was showing nicely. It was he who'd have to hurry, which was the only snag about being the one to create the diversion. Once things were properly under way he'd have to run for it, then drive like a bat out of hell to pick up Duke and N. farther down the coast—and pick up his share as well. It had not occurred to Basil Trenthorne that, with his employers' fondness for money and their propensity for causing accidents, he might be heading, once they were clear, for an accident himself. He threw away his cigarette, shook out a long dark robe from the parcel and slipped it over his head, then picked up the cumbersome goat's head mask and a flambeau and set off to rejoin Miss Seeton. Hilary Evelyn was taller and broader than Basil: the robe was too long and made him stumble. He hitched it up with the hand that held the torch, unaware that oil was spilling, soaking the cloth.

Miss Seeton looked at the black-robed figure in surprise. "Good gracious. What …?"

"I'll slip the mask on, light the torch and go on up, miss," he told her quietly. "You follow behind. I've put a couple of logs there to act as steps. Then have a good look at the people there and see if you can pick out anyone who was at the church."

"But …"

"Don't worry, miss," he encouraged her. "With me togged up like this they'll think you're part of the act." Would be too—the Virgin Sacrifice.

Miss Seeton would have made another protest but her companion laid the flambeau on the ground, lifted the goat's mask above his head and dropped it into place.

"Won't take long, miss," he mumbled through it. "Soon be over." Would be too, with all the shavings and twigs they'd packed underneath the branches. And with the edges soaked in paraffin there'd be a thin wall of flame all round in a moment, which'd hold her in place till the bonfire got going. That'd make her foot a caper or two—like a cat on hot bricks. Fun. Pity he couldn't stay to watch the end. The mask equally was made for a bigger man and Basil was finding vision difficult. He stooped for the torch, fumbled with matches and succeeded in lighting it at the second attempt. He moved forward with caution, grasping the robe with his free hand as his feet felt for the log steps. He found them and mounted. So—here went. The jig was on.

His arrival on the platform, with the blazing torch held high, was acclaimed with fervor by the members of the cult. Miss Seeton, who had followed and was trying to see past him, gazed in astonishment. Between thirty and forty men and women, masked as they had been at the church, fell on their knees and bowed their heads to the ground. They had been eating and drinking, but this was now abandoned. They staggered to their feet and, holding hands at arms' length, they began to weave counterclockwise around the rostrum in a stumbling caricature of a dance. Circling, they chanted:

"Tantalus and tantal me,
Tantal them and tantal thee.
Up one, down two, three or so—
Round and round about we go."

Well, really. Miss Seeton was shocked. Most of them had very few clothes on, and some none at all. So stupid. Apart from the silliness of the whole affair, on a late September night like this didn't they realize they'd catch bad colds? Still unsure what she was supposed to do, she looked to her companion for guidance. He ignored her and, stalking to the edge of the platform, brought his torch down in a sweeping gesture. A thin sheet of flame shot up from the parafined logs. He stepped back satisfied and turned, prepared to jump off at the rear. He would light that edge as he went, leaving the old cow boxed in by fire. Then he'd throw the torch to the center and the prepared twigs and shavings below the structure would set the whole thing going within seconds. If anyone ever did get on to what happened it could be put down to the old bag's nosiness in climbing up where she wasn't wanted, trying to have a look-see. Just an unfortunate accident.

Unfortunately for Basil Trenthorne, an accident had already occurred. His sweeping gesture had been his undoing. The torch had touched his robe: it had caught alight. The jig was on indeed and Basil footed it. His antics only worsened his condition. Punitive flames reared to envelop him: the papier-mâché mask began to burn. Shrieking, he slapped at his clothes. He dropped the flambeau and flung himself down, landing on the flame and smothering it. The torch went out, but not the man. Writhing and rolling in agony, he set fire to the shavings beneath the ill-secured branches.

The screams roused Miss Seeton from a moment of fascinated horror. Throwing down her handbag and umbrella, she dragged off her coat and flung it over him, trying to beat out the flames, but the flames forced her back. She must get help—at once: it would all be alight.... She looked about in desperation. Fire had raced round the oil-soaked edges and she stood as Basil had intended within four walls of flame. What were those idiotic people doing? She couldn't see them, but they must be there.... To reach them ... Something to protect her head—her coat was gone—what could she ...? She snatched up her umbrella, opened it and, holding it close before her face, ran to the side. At the edge the blast of heat made her falter. Forcing herself, she stepped forward into flame, she missed her footing and she fell.

Chapter 18

Potter was the first in the village to notice the distant glow. Restless at being taken off his beat, which although he had entire confidence in his colleagues he could never feel was performed with quite the same understanding and perspicacity as when carried out by himself, he had preferred to keep an eye on things by staying outside Sweetbriars and out of the way of the superintendent, who grew more grim as the hours passed. He went in and reported:

"Bonfire Iverhurst way, sir."

Delphick was indifferent. "Not unusual this time of year, is it?"

"No, sir. But 'twould be odd for them to be lighting it at midnight. May be no more'n a flare-up from one that was damped down, but there weren't a sign of one when I passed earlier. And a couple o' miles is far enough for a flare-up to be seen. Doesn't look to be near any of the farms—more south I'd say."

Midnight? The witching hour. A fire? Delphick's interest was roused. "Any way we can pinpoint it? I don't want to risk leaving here and being out of touch on some wild-goose chase."

"You could give Sir George a ring, sir. He's got a fine pair of glasses and from the attic of the Hall he'd locate it quick enough."

Delphick telephoned. While he waited for Sir George to ring him back he went up to Miss Seeton's bedroom, but even leaning out of the window at the rear he wasn't high enough to see more than a pink reflection in the sky. The telephone called him downstairs. Potter handed him the receiver.

"Sir George, sir."

Sir George was definite. "No bonfire, Superintendent— it's the wood by Iverhurst church, and from the look of it, spreading. I'm ringing the fire brigade. Need some blankets and staves for beating, and get out there meself. Tell Potter to stir up the village lads—may need 'em."

Delphick gave Potter the message. "Sir George seems worried. You know the conditions. How serious could it be?"

"Bad, sir. After three weeks of dry like we've had it'll go like kindling."

"Right. I'll ring headquarters while you rouse some men, and we'll be off."

The superintendent found that headquarters already had the news. Two of the mobile units had radioed and fire engines from Brettenden, from Ashford and from Rye were on their way. He hurried outside, to find the village was astir, with Potter giving the men instructions. People in hastily donned attire were coming from their houses; cars were being backed out of garages. A fire—and at Iverhurst— was far too good to miss. The Reverend Arthur Treeves, nightshirt tucked into trousers, a coat over all, bare feet in stout unmatching boots, trotted to Delphick's car, threw a horseblanket and a broom into the back and clambered after them.

"You'll give me a lift, Superintendent," he assumed.

Unwillingly Delphick nodded and started the engine. The reverend was too old for this. He glanced up. The sky was now hazed more orange than pink and turning red. Potter directed Stan Bloomer into the back with Arthur Treeves and leaped for the front seat as the car began to move. Behind them straggled a motley stream of cars and vans and bicycles. A message came through on Delphick's radio from Sergeant Ranger: bad fire about a mile inland. The Water Guards said it must be Iverhurst wood; spreading fast. Should he return or stay at Judy's Gap? Stay, Delphick decided. Get back to the boat and carry on with the patrol. If there was anybody at or under the church and his guess about the tunnel connecting with it was right, they might well break that way.

The superintendent parked off the road well short of the church, behind two patrol cars. Even at this distance he was inclined to question the cars' safety. The sight had been awe inspiring on their approach, with the old church outlined in defiance against the inferno of its traditional enemy. The roar of the furnace ahead of them had swallowed the beat of the car's engine, but when they pitched out and ran forward to join the four patrol officers at the far side of the grave-yard, who were beating with cut branches at upstart flames from sparks and debris carried on the wind, the effect was humbling. How could a man, or many, control an element? The drumming clamor was accented by the hiss and spit of oozing sap; the splintering, the crack, the crash as trees discarded tortured members.

The church? Delphick questioned. Searched and empty, he was told. The superintendent suppressed a feeling of sickness. If—if anyone had been in the wood when this started … and the speed at which it had spread … it was too late—far too late to worry anymore. Concentrate on what could be saved. The church. He still believed that somewhere below it or near it must be the Nuscientists' Secret Place. Try if it was possible to save the fools from roasting there.

People were arriving and forming into a line organized by Sir George. Women, many with children, were grouped at a distance to enjoy the fun. A police motorcyclist reported that a car was ablaze by the trees on the far side of the wood. He thought the car was empty but the heat had been too intense to make certain. He'd managed to read the number and it was the car there was a call out for and he'd wirelessed H.Q. The first of the fire engines arrived. Delphick, already smoke begrimed, his clothing singed, left his place to the motorcyclist and went to consult with the firemen's chief. What was the water situation? Bad enough; only the one well and little enough in that after weeks of dry. Best to concentrate on the church then, Delphick suggested.

Brinton drove up, followed by two more squad cars from Ashford, the men piling out to join the fire fighters.

"You heard about the car?" asked Brinton.

"Yes."

"She might've got out in time."

"Then where is she?"

Brinton eyed the conflagration. There was nothing more to say.

Miss Seeton got to her feet. How very stupid to have forgotten that she was on a platform and that there would be a drop. She might easily have twisted her ankle. She turned quickly to the rostrum and gasped. It was by now a swaying

184

mass of flame. It was—there was nothing—nothing that one—that anyone could do.

"Hey."

Startled out of her distress, Miss Seeton looked around. A young man buttoning his shirt and trying at the same time to pull on a jacket was running toward her.

"Hey," he repeated. "You're the one we tried to snatch the bag of. Miss Season or something."

"Seeton," corrected Miss Seeton automatically.

"You're in with the cops or some sort of cop yourself or something, aren't you?"

"No," said Miss Seeton.

"Look," he demanded eagerly, "when we get out of this— I'll show you the path we hacked to the church, and help all I can—will you put in a word for me? I'd nothing to do with it. I didn't bargain for any killing. I've nothing against the racket, and pinching money off the suckers, but murder ... I swear I knew nothing about it. Duke and N. must be crazy. Basil would never've tried it off his own bat. And then the silly fool goes and makes a bonfire of himself. There'll be one hell of a funk when Ma Trenthorne gets wind of it; they'll be handing out lifers all—"

Miss Seeton, who had understood little of this appeal, cut him short. "Do you mean to say you stood there and watched someone burn to death and did nothing to help?"

"How could I?" he protested. "I—I'd nothing on. And you followed him up there. I thought it meant a cop, that the gaff was blown, and we'd all be copped. I went for my clothes quick. By the time I cottoned to what the fool was up to it was too late. There'd been a tip that this was going to be a slap-up do with a virgin sacrifice and all the trimmings, but

I swear I thought it'd only be a chicken—they've used 'em before. If I'd …"

They? Miss Seeton had almost forgotten her surroundings in the shock of what had taken place. She looked about her. Men with animals' heads, women with masks, all half or wholly naked, still held hands and pranced around Basil's funeral pyre, still chanted:

"Up one, down two, three or so—
Round and round about we go."

"What's the matter with them?" She was incredulous. "They must be mad."

"Doped," the young man answered. "They don't know it but the wine is always spiked a bit to help them get the spirit of the thing; that's why I never touch it. I don't go for witch stuff and sabbaths. Me, I'm from Nuscience; I just came along for the ride and a bit o' free skirt."

"But," Miss Seeton expostulated, "they must have seen what happened. They—"

"They think it was meant: the sacrifice walks out of the fire and the Devil burns himself and then he'll 'come again.' Historical stuff. They're happy as be damned—think it's all for real."

There was a crash as the platform collapsed. Flames shot high and blazing wreckage was thrown among the happy damned. Undeterred, they capered on, apparently immune to burns; breaking hands to stoop and snatch up smoldering pieces, throwing them far and wide. Above them the trees had caught: now dried bracken in the undergrowth smoked, then broke to flame, igniting dead branches, drying leaves. Within moments fire was everywhere.

"For God's sake." The young man grabbed Miss Seeton's arm. "Come on, we've got to get out of this."

"But"—Miss Seeton looked at the madcap dancers—"we can't leave them here."

"Who cares? Let 'em burn if they want to; I'm off."

"You …" They couldn't leave. These people were sick, irresponsible. Somebody had to … Somehow she must make him help her. Help. She remembered. She faced him with authority. "You said you wanted my help with the police. Very well then, I will, if you'll help me now. But if you don't, I'll—I'll report you," she threatened.

He hesitated, moved and caught one of the women by the hand. "Come on," he shouted, "all of you. Out of this. Follow us."

The woman came to him willingly, clung to him, tried to make him dance; fumbled with the buttons of his shirt; putting her arms around him, she pressed herself against him. The pupils of her eyes were dilated, all sense of time, of place, direction as confused as was her ecstasy. They tried with one after another. All the members of the cult were docile, amorous and cloud-ridden, but always when released returned to their frenetic ritual.

"It's no good," the young man gasped, "we'll have to leave them."

Miss Seeton looked around in desperation. She had allowed the fire to stampede her once; now she must think. There must be some means, if only one could work it out logically and calmly. Her surroundings were not inducive either to logic or to calm. Improving on Mrs. Beeton's dictum, in her tome on household management, that fire can burn both up and down, this fire had spread in all directions. Except for the clearing in which they stood, fire was everywhere for as far as she could see. The whole wood by now appeared to be ablaze and the heat was becoming intolerable. These poor creatures seemed only to want to hold hands and dance. Very well, they should and she would lead them.

"Tie them together by the wrists," she ordered, "and put something for a lead on the front one that I can hold, then if I go ahead they'll have to follow me, and you stay at the back to keep them moving and make them stay in line."

Instinctively Miss Seeton had found the way to deal with him. Nuscience rules were strict and the youth was used to discipline, trained to obedience. The schoolmistress was accustomed to unruly children and some semblance of order soon emerged. The young man foraged, pulled laces from discarded shoes, found ties, tore clothing into strips. Looking down, Miss Seeton found that she still held the metal frame of her umbrella, to which clung scraps of melted nylon. She dropped the useless skeleton and, joining her new pupil, set to work. Between them they got their wayward company strung in line. An elastic belt from someone's trousers, tied round the wrist of the first woman they had caught, gave Miss Seeton the leading rein she needed.

"Now show me," she demanded, "this path you spoke of."

He pointed. To the south of the clearing an opening showed where a way had been hacked through the undergrowth. It was roofed and walled by fire: errant flames continually flicked across it. It was frightening; but by comparison it was clear and it was the only means of egress that they had. The young man took off his jacket and hung it over Miss Seeton's free arm.

"Use that to protect your face and for God's sake get going." He ran to the back to try to keep their charges in formation. Miss Seeton hesitated. Some word of encouragement she knew was needed, but all that came to her mind was the voice of the games mistress at the little school in Hampstead.

"Line up behind me," piped Miss Seeton, shrill but inaudible, "and *forward* STEP."

Progress was slow and erratic. The heat, the spitting and the crackling, the smoke, the smell of singeing cloth. The poor young man's coat … good cloth … seemed … waste … The pain from flames that licked at her hands and legs was fuzzling Miss Seeton's mind. All sense of urgency was gone and only deep-rooted determination kept her on her way. These silly people positively seemed to want to run into the fire. She had tried turning around to shout at the woman behind her, but her voice was drowned by the noise that raged about them and now she saved her breath since even shallow breathing in this inferno hurt one's chest. Her recruit, acting as whipperin, was up and down the line like some unpracticed sheepdog, snapping and snarling at intractable members of their flock. Thus, with Miss Seeton half running, stumbling at their head, this strange concourse, inspired by the example of the Devil, their master, caracoled and chanted through the hell of which they dreamed.

Chapter 19

Down in the Secret Place the atmosphere was becoming close, already a little hazy, heat and smoke were seeping through the air vents; there was a susurration, distant still, but growing; there was a suggestion of burning. The Nuscientists looked at each other, wide-eyed and questioning. Had it started? Was this the beginning of the end? How right they'd been: how right the Master. They gazed with satisfaction at the padlocked box, not unlike a coffin made of plastic, that held their valuables. As the noise and the smell of fire increased, they increased their practiced single-nostril breathing and their unpracticed prayers.

Mrs. Trenthorne looked about her. No Majordomes were present to comfort, to organize, advise. They must be attending on the Master, occupied in prayer, and of course, as a Trumpeter, Basil would be with them. A Serene too should be at the Master's side now that crisis was upon them. Since she alone of all this gathering was a Serene, her title—and the payment of five thousand pounds—entitled her, she felt, to pray in company with the hierarchy.

She moved to the far end of the chamber, wavered momentarily before invading the forbidden territory; then, rallying herself, determined, she turned the handle of the door.

The second chamber was empty. Where was the Master? Where the Majordomes? And where was Basil? At the far end a part of the stone wall was swung back, revealing a dark opening. She advanced upon it. Unfastening her handbag, she took out the flashlight they had all been advised to carry in case the lamps should fail. The beam showed her a narrow tunnel sloping downward. There was no question—none— no, none whatever, that the Master had deserted them. No. It was simply that she had misunderstood exactly where the Master's private quarters were. They must be farther down this passage. This second chamber would be only for the Majordomes—a kind of officers' mess—and quite unfit for the Master's meditations. Naturally they would be with him in his sanctum. Basil too. She would join them there. A mother's place should be at her son's side. She would join her prayers with theirs and assure the Master of her complete belief in his omniscience. And reassure herself.

In her progress down the passage Mrs. Trenthorne noted that the air was growing colder. She stopped when she came to the right-hand turn that led to the Downs, unsure which way to go, then ... she switched off her flashlight. She'd been right. Straight on, ahead of her, faintly, a light was showing. She listened. There was an echo of movement, more felt than heard. She switched on the flashlight again. Now that she was certain of her route she hurried. The light in front was brighter; soon she could see two men, each carrying a flashlight in one hand, with the other gripping by its handles, and straining under the weight, a ... a coffin? No. Now she recognized it. It was the box of valuables from the cave. Her money and her jewels were in that box. Appalled, she shouted:

"Stop." Furiously she repeated, "Stop, thieves." The rear man dropped the box and swung about. For an instant she saw his face—a stranger. She ran forward, screaming, "Thieves. Stop, thieves."

The beam from his flashlight was on her face, blinding her. There was an explosion. She halted in surprise, took a hesitant step, then pitched forward at his feet.

"You fool," flared N. "That'll be heard as far as the cave. They'll probably come after her, investigating."

"I had to crease her," snapped Duke. "She'd seen our faces."

"Why a gun? Just bash her brains in."

"We're nearly there. We'll be well clear before anybody'd get here. It doesn't matter."

But it did. Intent on argument and deafened by the report in a confined space, neither man had heard the pattering as earth and stones began to fall. The tunnel had not been built to withstand gun blast; moreover, it was old, in ill repair. The pattering crescendoed; the ceiling of the tunnel shuddered, cracked, the cracks widening and lengthening until a whole section of the roof smashed down on them.

The Customs officers, using night glasses, had picked up a boat stationed near the beach. They came in to inspect it. It proved to be a small motor launch with a shallow draft, and with the tide now on the ebb the depth of the water where it was anchored was little more than knee high. It was, they decided, a charter job, though what brought them to this conclusion Bob Ranger was unable to fathom. They tied alongside, boarded the launch and, as a precautionary measure, immobilized the engine. While they were thus engaged the sergeant waded ashore and was sitting on a boulder putting on his socks and shoes when faintly he heard cries followed by a muffled explosion. A few moments later there was a rumbling, then a thud, of which he could feel the vibration. By this time the Customs men had joined him. The three of them listened for any further indication, trying to gauge the point from which the noises had come. They judged that the last sounds that they had heard had been caused by an earth subsidence. The Water Guards clambered close in to the rock face underneath the overhanging scrub, stood back to back and held their flashlight beams steady in either direction, telling Bob to keep a lookout for dust. They waited; their patience was rewarded. A small, then a larger, cloud of dust billowed from among the rocks. They had found the entrance to the cave. Owing to the dust, breathing inside the cave was difficult, sight almost impossible, so a reconnaissance from above was determined upon until the air should clear. One officer stood guard at the cave's mouth, the other, with Bob, clambered straight up, forcing a way through the stunted bushes until they reached the top. They trekked inland, sweeping their lights in a wide swath until they came to the wound in the earth where the tunnel roof had collapsed. They started cautious excavations and almost immediately uncovered Duke's body. The man was dead: both back and neck were broken; a pistol was still clenched in a rigid hand. A voice appealed for help. They clawed at the ground and unearthed the end of a box; its gilt handle glittered in the flashlight beams. The box was heavy, long, like the plastic coffin of a child, and it took them time to pull it clear. Behind it N. moved. Bob lay down and caught him under the armpits to lift him free. N. screamed. One arm hung useless and some ribs were broken where the box had been driven into his side. Widening the gap, they gently eased him out and laid him by his dead companion. They were about to inspect his injuries when a sound between a snort and a moan arrested them. It came from a little farther on, beyond where the ground had fallen. Bob climbed down and saw the tunnel in front of him, only the bottom of it blocked by debris. He excavated, hand-shoveling the loose earth behind him until the way was clear. In the passage lay a woman. Despite the dust he recognized her: the one the Colveden family called Aunt Bray. At first sight she appeared to be unharmed, until he saw the hole in her coat above the left breast through which a trickle of blood was seeping. He knelt down to examine her. Revived by the light, she sat up suddenly, staring at him. In full voice she rasped:

"Thief. Thieves, all of you. My money ... my jewels—"

She hiccuped; stopped, surprised. Surprise and indignation remained frozen on her face as she went limp. Bob felt for a pulse: there was none. Aunt Bray had brayed her last.

Chapter 20

The fire was beating the beaters. The line had straggled as in twos and threes they were forced back across the churchyard. Foxon, with Sir George belaboring on one side and the Reverend Mr. Treeves patting his ineffectual best on the other, still held his place. They were helped by the fact that in front of them there was a break in the undergrowth as though a path had been cut into the wood, which prevented the fire from outflanking and surrounding them in their immediate vicinity. Looking up from his labors, Foxon stopped, incredulous. He blinked his watering, heat-seared eyes. Had there been …? No, just a trick of the … Nothing; no one could … There was—dear God, there was—movement ahead. He leaped around.

"Water," he yelled. "Water here, quick."

The nearest fireman caught the appeal, passed the word, misdirected his hose to where the detective constable was pointing, hit Foxon in the back and sent him sprawling, then raised his aim, and the only three other hoses left still spouting water joined with him to allow a steady curtain of rain to fall around the spot where the path from the wood emerged.

An infection of excitement rippled through the spectators. What were on? What did Sid Noakes want to go knocking that feller down with his hose for? This weren't no time for skylarking. What did they all want to put their water over there for? Little enough they'd got as 't was. T' old church she'd burn down now for sure. Something were up. Everyone, even the begrimed men slaving to control the fire's advance, paused to watch and wonder at this new development. The church roof, as though jealous of this sudden diversion of attention, ceased smoldering and began to blaze in earnest. To the enthrallment of the beholders, through the dripping veil which fell from the firemen's triumphal arch, indistinct, then clearcut in the orange glare, appeared Miss Seeton and her cavorting crew. The church roof, admitting defeat, dramatically enhanced its rival's entrance by collapsing in thunder and a shower of sparks.

The soaked Foxon scrambled to his feet. For a second he stared, still disbelieving: this was his charge, a charge on which he'd fallen down—asleep; this was the one that he'd been ordered to protect, the one who, gamely trying, had ended by protecting—saving—both herself and him; this was the one ... A surge of relief, exultancy, carried him forward. He gathered her up.

"You—" He could find no more words. "You, you—" he burbled.

Avidly the villagers drank in the scene. Well, they'd always said, and now 't were proved, 't were witch's work. No one but 'er could do a thing like that, come walkin' through a fire with all 'er friends. And what'd they been up to in the first place all naked and shameless and prancing about? Just like t' Bible 't were or a fillum, poppin' in and out of fiery furnaces

196

cool as cucumbers and no 'arm done. As Mrs. Flax pronounced, couldn't be nought but devil's work. Under the titillation of horrified disapproval they began to feel an upgrowth of civic pride. No other village, no, nor town for that, had got one'd do the things she did. She'd got 'em all bamboozled right enough, police an' all. Look at that Foxon over t' Ashford huggin' 'er an' throwin' 'er about. Whatever next?

Despite Miss Seeton's protests, Foxon, responsible once again for safe deliverance, carried her with pride to meet his advancing superiors. He set her down in front of Delphick and Brinton and stood back panting and beaming like a puppy which had retrieved its first bird. Delphick's feelings were mixed. How she had the gall to get him worked into such a lather, until in common sense he'd had to write her off. And then to saunter calmly out of the middle of her own cremation at the head of a gaggle of performing apes. A good hiding was what she needed. Speechless, he compromised with a tight grip on both her hands and, unobservant for once, failed to notice that she winced.

"Oh, Superintendent"—Miss Seeton was grieved—"and Mr. Brinton too, I am so truly sorry about that young policeman. I'm afraid he was killed. Quite dreadful. And I—I wasn't very helpful, I'm afraid. It was all so quick. But really there was nothing one could do. I think he got carried away with all the dressing up and playacting. And he would wave that lighted torch about—so dangerous—and set himself alight. If only," she regretted, "he'd warned me, I would have been firm."

"What young policeman?" asked Delphick.

"The one Mr. Brinton sent to fetch me for the identification. Though"—she eyed the chief inspector with severity—"I think you should have realized that one cannot identify people wearing masks."

"He wasn't a policeman," exploded Brinton, "and I didn't send him."

"Oh, yes, indeed he was," Miss Seeton contradicted. "He said so. And he said you had. And besides, he was in uniform. And if he wasn't, he wouldn't have been." Unexpectedly she sat down on the grass. Concerned, Delphick dropped to his knees beside her. She looked at him in bewilderment. "I'm so sorry, Superintendent. I think … I think, perhaps, I'm just a little tired."

Dr. Knight, kneeling on her other side, examined the blisters on her hands, applied ointment, gauze and bandages.

"Glad to hear you admit it for once." He eased off her wet shoes and stockings and treated burns on her legs and feet. He scanned her face. "No trouble there. You were luckier than you deserve."

"Oh, no," explained Miss Seeton, "that was the young man. He wrapped his coat round my arm to protect my face." She turned to Delphick. "He was most helpful. He's not really one of these strange people who wear masks. He belongs to that other odd religion." She looked up at Brinton. "The Maidstone one, I mean. And was only there tonight because—well, not, I fear, from quite the best of motives." She put a bandaged hand on Delphick's sleeve. "But he said he'd no idea about a murder. That would be poor Mrs. Paynel, I suppose; he assured me that he wouldn't stand for it. And without him I really don't know what we should have done. I could never have managed on my own. Nor did I know the path: he showed it to me." For a moment she was back in the clearing with the wood ablaze all around her.

Her mind blurred. Yes, now she came to think of it, she really must admit that she was tired. And the young man had been brave, because there was no denying he'd been frightened. He could have run away. Her eyes focused on Delphick in appeal. "But he didn't, you see. When he could have. I think, after all, we should remember that."

The set of Delphick's mouth relented. He grasped her purpose if not the meaning of her words. "We'll remember," he promised her.

Brinton took a mental inventory. Replace: one umbrella, missing; one hat, charred; one coat, one suit—replace the whole caboodle. But worth it. Irregular she might be, but somehow she always seemed to bring it off. He glanced across to where Sir George clung to Miss Seeton's leading rein, which he had grabbed when her troupe, deprived of their leader, had promptly headed back toward the fire. He stood there dogged and determined while his adopted team gyrated round him and Miss Seeton's late assistant, with Foxon, tried to sort them out in vain. Brinton eyed the dancers' exposed and kippered flesh. All right, so she did bring home the bacon—home cured, at that.

Dr. Knight stood up. "Good. That'll do. Now you're off to bed." He signaled to two stretcher bearers. "Anne can ride back with you to the nursing home, get you to bed and give you something to make you sleep."

"I—"

"No argument. You're doing as you're told for once. I'll have a look at you in the morning."

"No." Lady Colveden had joined them. "You'll have your hands and your nursing home full enough as it is. Miss Seeton's coming back with us—Anne can help me get her to bed—and she'll have two large helpings of porridge, brown sugar and cream; sustaining, good for the digestion and better for sleep than all your pills. And don't make it too early in the morning; let's hope she sleeps on. The stretcher can go in the back of the estate wagon, and we'll get off as soon as I can collect Nigel and if you"—she appealed to the police officers—"can rescue George from acting as a maypole in that striptease show."

The ambulance men bore Miss Seeton away and the rest of the group went also, to the relief of Sir George.

"Oh," exclaimed Lady Colveden on closer view, "poor wretches, they must be in the most dreadful pain."

"Not yet," replied the doctor, "though unless we get them under sedation and treated soon, they will be."

"Doped?" queried Delphick.

"Not necessarily. Though I wouldn't be surprised if they'd had a mild dose of LSD to start them off. But from the look of it I'd call this a classic example of self-hypnosis or mass-induced hysteria. They worship the Devil and hellfire, so fire attracts them like moths to flame. They're impervious to pain and can't even feel it when their wings are singed." He moved in among them, took the belt from Sir George and handed it to one of the ambulance attendants who had followed them. "Lead them over there," he ordered. "And you and the others can hold them still while I give them each a shot to quieten them. How many ambulances are there?"

"Four, doctor."

"See if you can call up more. If not, take 'em in relays. The worst cases'd better go to the Ashford General and we'll see what can be done."

Lady Colveden watched them led away; listened to the words they sang as they gamboled with faltering steps after their new keeper.

"Up the mountain, up the peak.
Ups-a-daisy, up the creek.
Up one, down two, three or so—
Round and round about we go."

"But at least," she decided, "they'll have learned their lesson. They won't be so silly again."

"I doubt that, Lady Colveden." Delphick's tone was dry. "The wise increase in wisdom, but folly follows its own guise."

"They're just plain off their chumps, sir," Foxon volunteered. "All that cuckoo they keep singing—plain cuckoo."

"Yes?" Delphick lifted an eyebrow. "It's one of the traditional chants. Try substituting the original possessive pronouns for the definite and indefinite articles and you may get the gist of it."

Foxon frowned and started muttering. Then his face cleared and he laughed. "Oh—I get it, sir," he enthused. "Pretty filthy, isn't it. It's …" He remembered Lady Colveden's presence. "That's to say … I mean … yes …" His voice trailed off.

Delphick sized up Miss Seeton's helper. "You, I gather, are one of the Nuscience lot?"

"Er—yes, a Trumpeter." He wilted at Delphick's expression and answered the unspoken question. "We're sort of public relations, arrange all the ads, things like that. Get the foo—the people interested and explain things. Or explain 'em away," he admitted.

"Good. Then you should be able to explain a few things to us. Such as exactly what happened in the wood."

The young man looked scared. "Honestly, sir, there wasn't anything to be done. Trenthorne dressed himself up as the Devil, climbed onto the platform followed by the old lady and then his clothes caught fire and it was all over in a second. I don't know how she got out of it herself."

"I see." Delphick thought. "I do see. It sounds as if our Basil intended Miss Seeton to be the Virgin Sacrifice and the trick backfired on him."

"Yes," the boy agreed, "something like that. Sort of thing they believe in, but generally they use a cock or hen. And after that we couldn't do anything with them. If it hadn't been for her they'd all've burned. She … she's pretty good, you know. Because seeing her walk out of it and Trenthorne burned, the others—well, they enjoyed it, it sent them crazy."

"Yes," assented Delphick, "I can see it might."

"You mean," exploded Brinton, "that lot actually enjoys roasting people?"

"Not quite, Chris. As far as I get the hang of it, most religions have something of the kind—death of the deity and resurrection. In witchcraft there was the seven-year cycle with the godhead as a burnt offering, only to rise like the phoenix from his own ashes." He eyed the Trumpeter directly. "And another thing you can explain is the secret of the Secret Place. We'll patch you up and then we'll be taking you in and we'll need a statement—a full statement. The fuller the better for you." The boy started to protest. "I understand from Miss Seeton that you were helpful—helped to save her and the others from the fire at some risk to yourself. We'll be taking note of that too."

Relieved, the youth leaned forward eagerly. "The Secret Place, sir. It's here in the cellars below the church. If it can be cleared I'll show the way in through the crypt. You push a stone and a bit of the wall swings open like a door. They must all still be there if they're not charred to cinders."

Delphick and Brinton got things organized. The fire chief judged that the wood could do little further damage and should be left to burn itself out; but he forbade anyone to approach the red-hot shambles that had been a church. Three of the water tenders would be returning shortly with new supplies. Others would fetch more, and they'd douse the ruins until they were cool enough to be investigated with danger only from tottering walls and beams. But there could be no hope of getting near the crypt before the morning. So that those who were not immediately concerned had better get some rest and food and then be back by dawn, when they could help to clear the wreckage.

Dawn broke on a clear September morning to wipe away the shadows and the turmoil of the night. The villagers were back, bringing cheer for the weary, sweating men who had toiled to clear the still-steaming ruins. They plied them with bread and cheese, with egg and bacon sandwiches, with homemade pies, with flasks of black and sweetened tea and fizzy drinks of varied colors; they offered them cakes and ale.

The news had spread and crowds were gathering. Neighboring villagers, local townsfolk, people from near, from far, all thronged to see the outcome. Well to the fore, representatives from the newspapers, press photographers and two television crews jostled for position. Balked by the absence of Miss Seeton, who still slept, they centered their attention and their cameras on a long padlocked plastic box, coffin-shaped and with a handle at each end, over which stood guard Bob Ranger and two members of the uniformed police. Speculation was rife. The first of the bodies to be brought out of the church? Another murder? A confrontation of the killer with his victim? They pressed the police, bombarded everyone with questions, but got no satisfaction. Then at last the way was clear and, led by the firemen, Delphick and Brinton with the young Trumpeter, followed by Dr. Knight and two ambulance men, picked their way down into the crypt.

The scene which confronted them when they entered the cellar resembled Hogarth's impression of the debtors' prison. It jarred them to find that they were not welcome saviors. Some of the inmates were in shock, induced by their realization of the world's finale; brought home to them by the crashes that they had heard, the heat they had endured and the fumes of fire that they had breathed throughout their night-long vigil. Some were apathetic, all disbelieving, and the exhortations of their rescuers made no impression.

The Trumpeter whispered to Delphick, "They know me. May I try, sir?" Delphick nodded. The young man strode forward. "Come on," he snapped. "Up. Out of this, the lot of you."

Someone they recognized, the tone of command, the authority they craved, brought a response and brought them to their feet. With assistance and cajoling, with kindness and coercion they were chivied up and out into the daylight.

Their appearance was greeted by a cheer and the whir of television cameras: microphones were rushed toward them in order that no word of their message of thanksgiving for their safe deliverance should be lost to the world at large.

The long ordeal was ended; the night of fear was over; the threat of Armageddon passed; the burden of responsibility for the making of a New World had been lifted from their shoulders. Behind them lay the blackened defilement of the church and wood: before them the Kent countryside glowed green under a blue sky flecked with white clouds gilt-edged by the new day's sun, the golden glint repeated upon earth, where the first touch of autumn was tinting the leaves. Their homes were safe; their families, their friends yet lived. A row of smiling faces welcomed them. Their valuables would be restored, the box containing them was there on view.

They gazed dumbfounded: a feeling too great to be repressed, almost too deep for utterance began to bud, to swell, to burgeon, to well up until it blossomed into words from the most articulate, the most affected member of the group.

"It's all too disappointing really," said Mrs. Blaine.

Preview

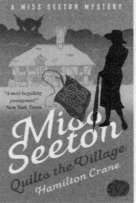

It's practically a Royal Marriage! The highly eligible son of Miss Seeton's old friends Sir George and Lady Colveden has wed the daughter of a French count.

Miss Seeton lends her talents to the village scheme to create a quilted 'Bayeux Tapestry' for Nigel and his bride. But her intuitive sketches reveal a startlingly different perspective—involving buried Nazi secrets, and links to a murdered diplomat and a South American dictator …

Serene amidst every kind of skulduggery, this eccentric English spinster steps in where Scotland Yard stumbles, armed with nothing more than her sketchpad and umbrella!

The new Miss Seeton mystery

COMING SOON!

About the Miss Seeton series

Retired art teacher Miss Seeton steps in where Scotland Yard
stumbles. Armed with only her sketch pad and umbrella, she
is every inch an eccentric English spinster and at every turn
the most lovable and unlikely master of detection.

Further titles in the series—

Picture Miss Seeton
A night at the opera strikes a chord of danger when
Miss Seeton witnesses a murder ... and paints a portrait
of the killer.

Miss Seeton Draws the Line
Miss Seeton is enlisted by Scotland Yard when her paintings
of a little girl turn the young subject into a model for murder.

Witch Miss Seeton
Double, double, toil and trouble sweep through the village
when Miss Seeton goes undercover ... to investigate a local
witches' coven!

Miss Seeton Sings
Miss Seeton boards the wrong plane and lands amidst a
gang of European counterfeiters. One false note, and her
new destination is deadly indeed.

Odds on Miss Seeton
Miss Seeton in diamonds and furs at the roulette table?
It's all a clever disguise for the high-rolling spinster ... but
the game of money and murder is all too real.

Miss Seeton, By Appointment
Miss Seeton is off to Buckingham Palace on a secret
mission—but to foil a jewel heist, she must risk losing the
Queen's head ... and her own neck!

Advantage, Miss Seeton
Miss Seeton's summer outing to a tennis match serves up more than expected when Britain's up-and-coming female tennis star is hounded by mysterious death threats.

Miss Seeton at the Helm
Miss Seeton takes a whirlwind cruise to the Mediterranean—bound for disaster. A murder on board leads the seafaring sleuth into some very stormy waters.

Miss Seeton Cracks the Case
It's highway robbery for the innocent passengers of a motor coach tour. When Miss Seeton sketches the roadside bandits, she becomes a moving target herself.

Miss Seeton Paints the Town
The Best Kept Village Competition inspires Miss Seeton's most unusual artwork—a burning cottage—and clears the smoke of suspicion in a series of local fires.

Hands Up, Miss Seeton
The gentle Miss Seeton? A thief? A preposterous notion—until she's accused of helping a pickpocket … and stumbles into a nest of crime.

Miss Seeton by Moonlight
Scotland Yard borrows one of Miss Seeton's paintings to bait an art thief … when suddenly *a second* thief strikes.

Miss Seeton Rocks the Cradle
It takes all of Miss Seeton's best instincts—maternal and otherwise—to solve a crime that's hardly child's play.

Miss Seeton Goes to Bat
Miss Seeton's in on the action when a cricket game leads to mayhem in the village of Plummergen … and gives her a shot at smashing Britain's most baffling burglary ring.

Miss Seeton Plants Suspicion
Miss Seeton was tending her garden when a local youth was arrested for murder. Now she has to find out who's really at the root of the crime.

Starring Miss Seeton
Miss Seeton's playing a backstage role in the village's annual Christmas pageant. But the real drama is behind the scenes ... when the next act turns out to be murder!

Miss Seeton Undercover
The village is abuzz, as a TV crew searches for a rare apple, the Plummergen Peculier—while police hunt a murderous thief ... and with Miss Seeton at the centre of it all.

Miss Seeton Rules
Royalty comes to Plummergen, and the villagers are plotting a grand impression. But when Princess Georgina goes missing, Miss Seeton herself has questions to answer.

Sold to Miss Seeton
Miss Seeton accidentally buys a mysterious antique box at auction ... and finds herself crossing paths with some very dangerous characters!

Sweet Miss Seeton
Miss Seeton is stalked by a confectionary sculptor, just as a spate of suspicious deaths among the village's elderly residents calls for her attention.

Bonjour, Miss Seeton
After a trip to explore the French countryside, a case of murder awaits Miss Seeton back in the village ... and a shocking revelation.

Miss Seeton's Finest Hour
War-time England, and a young Miss Emily Seeton's suspicious sketches call her loyalty into question—until she is recruited to uncover a case of sabotage.

About the author

Heron Carvic was an actor and writer, most recognisable today for his voice portrayal of the character Gandalf in the first BBC Radio broadcast version of *The Hobbit*, and appearances in several television productions, including early series of *The Avengers* and *Dr Who*.

Born Geoffrey Richard William Harris in 1913, he held several early jobs including as an interior designer and florist, before developing a successful dramatic career and his public persona of Heron Carvic. He only started writing the Miss Seeton novels in the 1960s, after using her in a short story.

Heron Carvic died in a car accident in Kent in 1980.

Note from the Publisher

While he was alive, series creator Heron Carvic had tremendous fun imagining Emily Seeton and the supporting cast of characters.

In an enjoyable 1977 essay Carvic recalled how, after having first used her in three short stories, "Miss Seeton upped and demanded a book"—and that if "she wanted to satirize detective novels in general and elderly lady detectives in particular, he would let her have her head ..."

You can now **read one of those first Miss Seeton short stories** and **Heron Carvic's essay in full**, as well as receive updates on further releases in the series, by signing up at http://farragobooks.com/miss-seeton-signup